GET REAL #2

Girl Reporter Sinks School!

GET REAL

SERIES

GET REAL #1:
Girl Reporter Blows Lid off Town!

GET REAL #2:
Girl Reporter Sinks School!

eal the game- positive sign. Despite the loss N.Y.S.A.I.S tournament. With four [illegible]
! It was a great the Dutchmen proved able to a third place finish in the beat the
hey played its play with the near undefeated league, the Dutchmen found Zeffin [illegible]
proved strong. Falcons of Rivermont. Also themselves [illegible] if they upset. C

GET REAL #2

Girl Reporter Sinks School!

Created by

LINDA ELLERBEE

HarperCollins*Publishers*

were all geared lowed Stampar to get zero have some momentum going turned to
[illegible] power goals, and seemed to knock into the tournament. I am the [illegible]
lake. Riverdale the superstar out of his game. proud that we got here, and I stepped
dominate the "Tom played huge for us. He think that if we play as a team know ho
the dominant shut down the best player in we will be able to play with [illegible]

J

My deepest thanks to Katherine Drew, Anne-Marie Cunniffe, Lori Seidner, Whitney Malone, Roz Noonan, Alix Reid and Susan Katz, without whom this series of books would not exist. I also want to thank Christopher Hart, whose book, *Drawing on the Funny Side of the Brain*, retaught me how to cartoon. At age 11, I was better at it than I am now. Honest.

Drawings by Linda Ellerbee

 Printed in the United States of America. For information address HarperCollins Children's Books, a division of HarperCollins Publishers, 10 East 53rd Street, New York, NY 10022.
http://www.harperchildrens.com

Library of Congress Cataloging-in-Publication Data
Ellerbee, Linda.
Girl reporter sinks school! / created by Linda Ellerbee.
p. cm. — (Get real ; #2)
Summary: Eleven-year-old Casey Smith decides to do an investigative story for the school paper about a cheating ring operating on campus.
ISBN 0-06-440756-X (pbk.) — ISBN 0-06-028246-0 (lib. bdg.)
[1. Cheating—Fiction. 2. Journalism—Fiction. 3. Schools—Fiction.] I. Title. II. Series: Ellerbee, Linda. Get real ; #2.
PZ7.E42845Gi 2000 99-30306
[Fic]—dc21 CIP
AC

Typography by Carla Weise
1 2 3 4 5 6 7 8 9 10
❖
First Edition

For the kids,
who always get real

Girl Reporter Sinks in Sea of Success

I'M CASEY SMITH, and life just isn't fair. Have you noticed? I know, you hear adults tell you that all the time. Usually when some dorky teacher gives you major homework on a Friday. But this time I'm taking it personally.

Just last week I wrote the biggest scoop in the history of Trumbull Middle School's newspaper, *Real News*. Journalistically speaking, I blew the lid off this town.

Not bad for an eleven-year-old girl.

Believe me when I tell you that the story was a sensation. And believe me when I tell you there isn't a whole lot of sensational stuff going on here in Abbington, which is a pretty small town in some pretty small mountains called the Berkshires, in western Massachusetts. Watching leaves change color is about as exciting as it gets.

So I wrote this whopper of a story. I say this with total modesty, of course. Then comes the unfair part. I had to do it all over again—in one week!

Everybody was saying things like "Way to go!" and "Can't wait to read your next scoop, Casey!" You'd think I'd be able to relax for a minute. Well, guess what? The paper comes out every week, and deadlines come at you like a 18-wheeler on a downhill skid.

Usually I have a million ideas for stories. But now my brain was full of that fuzz on your TV when the cable goes out. I'd never been the type to choke under pressure, but I was choking, big-time.

On Tuesday, I headed for the before-school status meeting of the staff of *Real News*. Today I was supposed to present my brilliant story ideas to our editor-in-chief, the terminally perky Megan O'Connor.

It was a rainy September morning. My wet sneakers squished as I trudged down the hall. Every damp footstep reminded me that my brain was waterlogged, too. Was it too late to suddenly develop an acute case of laryngitis? Strep foot?

When I got to the *Real News* room, I stopped in the doorway, surprised. The room was about the size of a closet. And now, it was crammed with students—all sixth graders, like me.

Bobbing over their heads was Mr. Baxter, my English teacher and the newspaper's advisor. I had completely forgotten that he was bringing one of his English classes to observe our meeting.

Talk about pressure! Suddenly a newspaper headline flashed through my head. They do that a lot. It's the work of the creep who lives inside my brain. The one who whispers in my ear: You're gonna fail.

REAL NEWS GETS PUBLISHED WITHOUT CASEY SMITH

Even though the meeting hadn't started, the staff was hard at work. Toni Velez, our photographer, was examining a contact sheet through a loupe. Orange curls exploded from her ponytail and spilled over the sheet. Toni is like one of those models who spends hours arranging her hair to make it look as though she just got up. But I wouldn't say anything about it to her. The girl has a serious 'tude. You do not, I repeat *do not*, want to mess with Toni.

Gary Williams, sports reporter, was hunched over his laptop, his lucky baseball cap swung backward on his head. Gary likes to think he's a major jock, but he's really more of a jock wannabe. His friends are the ones who are actually driving in the runs and scoring the touchdowns.

I have to admit that Gary is cute, or at least the girls at Trumbull think so. He has caramel-colored eyes and skin the color of coffee with a big serving of cream stirred in. But he's also one of the most boring guys I know. If you ever see him coming at you down the hall, run. If not, you'll get a play-by-play description of *Monday Night Football.*

My pal Ringo, The Truly Weird, was busy pinning up cartoons he'd drawn about his character, Simon, for the class to look at. Ringo invented the "Simon Says" feature for our issue last week.

Actually, we sort of invented the entire newspaper last week. But that's another story. Old news.

Back to Ringo. I can usually count on him to space out on obligations as well as the basic facts of the universe. But today even spaced-out, tie-dyed Ringo was more on the ball than I was.

So what was I going to do? Cop to my lack of ideas? Apologize to the gang and grovel like a slug?

Let me clue you in. Groveling is not my style.

"Casey! You're here. Super!" Megan beckoned to me from across the room. The blue in her sweater matched her canvas backpack, as well as the hair band that swept back her shoulder-length blond hair.

Wardrobe coordination is key for me, too. Today, the mud splatter on my jeans exactly matched the color of my eyes. Not that Megan would have seen it that way. No, not Megan. To use one of Megan's own favorite adjectives, she's super. Super-organized. Super-dedicated. Super-Pain-in-the-Butt. Got it? But here's her major problem. She's also a super editor-in-chief.

Well, maybe that's not *her* problem. Maybe it's mine. Because *I* had wanted to be editor of the paper. And yet, somehow, I had ended up voting for Megan to be editor-in-chief. I had realized, through circumstances too painful to explain here, that I was a better reporter than editor. I knew that. But I didn't have to *like* it.

"Isn't this great?" Megan said, indicating the crowd. "A couple of kids told me they want to write stories for the paper. You know that series we're doing on school clubs and how they relate to real life?"

I rolled my eyes. The idea had sent me to snooze-city, but Megan was stuck on it. I like stories that grab you by the throat and shake you like a bulldog. Megan likes stories that *relate.*

"Casey, you know my friends, right?" Megan continued cheerfully. One day Megan O'Connor will be the world's first person to be arrested for an excess of good cheer. Or at least, let's hope so.

She indicated the girls standing with her.

"Sure," I said, "I know them." Even though I didn't know their names. We were all new to Trumbull, since this was our first year in middle school. But Megan's friends were interchangeable, anyway. They all had shiny hair. Shiny eyes. Shiny teeth. Shiny brains. Shiny rhymes with whiny, doesn't it? No accident there. *And*—they were all color-coordinated.

"This is Phoebe Trippett and Jessica Rundel and Kelli Catrice," Megan said, nodding around the circle. "Guys, you know Casey Smith, right? She broke that super story about the paper mill?"

The girls and I exchanged hellos. Lukewarm all around. Jessica turned away with a shake of her shiny auburn mane. Talk about the cold shoulder. Either that or she was practicing her lion-queen imitation.

The shiny hair theme continued with Phoebe and Kelli. Phoebe wore a red sweater that matched her red rain boots. Kelli wore a gold necklace with a little heart, and her blouse had heart-shaped buttons. Really. I kid you not. Even though I didn't know these girls, I knew their type. They belong to about fifty clubs *and* they maintain a straight-A average. And in their spare time, they take ballet, gymnastics, pottery, yoga, piano, painting, riding, swimming, skating and modeling-for-beginners. They make me very, very, very tired.

"Kelli is a super athlete," Megan said. "She's hoping to make the cheerleading squad. And Phoebe and Jessica and I all went to Millridge Elementary together. They thought about joining our staff, but opted for the debating squad."

"And the French Club," Phoebe added.

I looked from one shiny-haired girl to the other. Even after that rundown from Megan, it was still hard to tell them apart.

Megan turned to me. "Phoebe's article in our series on school clubs is called 'How to Win Every Argument.' She's learning all kinds of skills from the debating squad."

"Actually, I brought a draft for you to see this morning," Phoebe said.

"Terrific," I said, almost politely.

"Toni took pictures of the debating squad already, so it's really shaping up," Megan bubbled on. She glanced at the clock. "Oops! I'd better start the meeting. Let's all head for Dalmatian Station."

"Dalmatian what?" Kelli asked.

"It's our table," I said, pointing to the polka-dotted table with green legs in the corner. "It was donated by Megan's grandmother's attic. Ringo called it Dalmatian Station, and the name stuck."

"Okay, class, settle down," Mr. Baxter called above the din as the staff took seats around the polka-dotted table. "We're here to observe how a newspaper gets put together."

Our staff room wasn't exactly designed for crowds, so Mr. Baxter's class had to find seats on the floor. When they had all squeezed in somewhere, they looked up at us expectantly, as if we were going to burst into song.

Megan looked a little nervous as she consulted her notepad. "Okay," she began. "Our drop-dead deadline for finished stories is after school on Thursday. The paper has to be laid out and put to bed before lunch on Friday. We do that on computers. Then, over the weekend, our final layout goes to the printer. Then, on Monday morning, *Real News* gets handed out. But first, we have to fill the paper with stories. And that's what this meeting's about. Gary, what do you have cooking?"

"A story on Cal Pillson," Gary said. "He's probably the most awesome athlete Trumbull has."

"What's the hook?" Megan asked. Every story needs a twist—a hook—the angle that makes it a story. Anyone who works for a newspaper knows that. You don't even have to be little miss know-it-all.

"He's equally amazing in football and basketball," Gary said. "But when the seasons overlap, he's overloaded. His coaches are leaning on him pretty hard to choose one or the other. Should he have to? Why? And when? Can't he wait until high school to choose?"

Megan nodded. "I like it."

"This guy's got game like you can't believe," Gary went on. "His layup is supreme."

"Football is awesome to watch," Ringo said, nodding. "Like hip-hop with shoulder pads."

Gary rolled his eyes. "I was talking *basketball*, space cadet."

Ringo nodded. "Ah. Right. You know what I love? How they catch the ball with their heads. You know . . ." Ringo's shaggy hair swung wildly as he pantomimed bumping a ball with his head.

I laughed along with everyone else. "Hey, Ringo, you've invented a new dance craze," I said, imitating him. We both bobbed our heads in unison.

"Excuse me," Gary said, pained. "Do you mean *soccer*?"

"Right!" Ringo snapped his fingers. "I knew that. I think. But basketball reminds me of soccer, somehow. Maybe because they both have goalies."

Gary winced. "Didn't your dad teach you anything about sports?"

"Nah," Ringo said. "But he did get me into Zen and the art of skateboard maintenance."

Gary stared at Ringo as though he'd been beamed down from Jupiter, which is, come to think of it, probably not far off the mark.

Grinning, Megan turned to Toni. "Toni? What else have you got besides the debating squad photos?"

Toni was in the middle of refastening the high ponytail that made her hair spew from her head like a water fountain. She pointed to a contact sheet with her chin. "I shot those before-and-afters for the photo essay."

"Before and after?" Gary asked.

"A photo essay on what the school looks like before we get here, and after we leave," Toni explained. "Megan's idea."

Gary and I leaned over Megan's shoulder and squinted at the sheet. Toni might be full of herself, but at least she knows her way around a lens.

"These shots are super," Megan exclaimed.

Gary grinned. "Sunrise on the athletic field? Cool."

"I had to get up way too early for that one," Toni complained.

"And the cafeteria after lunch looks pretty scary," Ringo said.

Toni cracked a smirk. "I thought we could caption it something like 'After Feeding Time.'"

"Super!" Megan beamed at everybody. I don't know how she does that, much less *why*. She then looked at the cartoons Ringo had tacked to the walls. "Ringo, I can see you've been busy. I like all the cartoons. But let's wait to vote on them until the issue shapes up. Now—let's hear from Casey."

I could feel every pair of eyes from Mr. Baxter's class fasten on me. My throat felt like sandpaper and my palms were damp. Okay, I get nervous, just like anyone else. But you'd never be able to tell. That's because I'm so awesome at disguise. Turn up the volume and the attitude, and don't let anybody see you sweat.

I swallowed. "I think I've come up with another great article," I said. It was amazing how confident I sounded! "An in-depth study of how the U.S. Congress works. I mean, the Congress is back in session, just like school. I can tie it into our Student Council. Kids are really into responsible government, Megan."

Megan looked cautious. "It sounds like an interesting *feature*," she said. "But not the front page. And I'm not sure how the Congress angle relates to the average student at Trumbull. . . ."

Megan was always jawing about the "average student." It really fried my cheese. A newspaper is supposed to take on tough issues. Wake people up. "Okay fine," I said. "How about an in-depth article on Baby Spice vs. Posh?"

A few guys snickered.

Megan ignored my biting sarcasm. "How about the computer upgrade at the library? That's news."

"Whoa, a spellbinder," I said.

Toni snorted. "I'm with you, girl," she muttered.

"And they're reseeding the athletic field," Megan said, checking her notepad.

"Great," I said. "World-shaking events are taking place every single day, and you want me to write about *grass*."

This time, everyone laughed. Megan's face flushed. She flipped her notebook closed. Maybe I'd gone a tad over the line. Maybe. But you wouldn't hear me say so out loud.

"Okay. I'll leave it up to you to come up with something brilliant," she said. "If not, I think the library story is the way to go. I'd like to hear your *new* story idea by tomorrow, please."

It was a standoff. Everyone in the room looked at me.

"I'll have it by lunch today," I shot back, digging myself in deeper. Very deep. Any deeper and I'd hit bedrock.

Incredible Leaking Brain Still Oozing

I REGRETTED WHAT I'd said as I headed for my first-period class. Sometimes my mouth gets ahead of my brain. I shouldn't have kept cracking jokes at Megan's expense. Especially in front of her friends. But she put me on the spot!

Now I had to be brilliant by lunchtime, and my morning was filled with the awful necessity of going to classes. I couldn't space out, either. I had a math test coming up on Friday, and I had to pay attention. Mr. Lanigan didn't get the nickname Terminator for nothing.

Math whipped along at cruise control until I hit a speed bump. I'd forgotten to bring my homework to class, but it was in my locker. For once, Terminator let me slide. If I slipped it in his mailbox by fourth-period lunch, I was golden.

Well, okay. Probably not golden. I'd done my homework, but I was still a little lost in math. Wait—maybe there was a story there. Students who suddenly hit a logjam in a subject . . .

On second thought . . . nah.

"Tell me about it," Andy Chong said to me after class when I confessed my cluelessness.

Troy Chandler overheard us. "I'm in the same boat," he said. "The test is going to be brutal. Do you think you'll pass?"

"I've got it covered," I said confidently. I don't like to admit any weakness. Especially to boys.

"It's doubtful." Andy sighed. "I'm going to study my brains out, starting tonight."

Troy widened his eyes and shuddered. "Andy Chong: The Incredible Leaking Brain! Eeeeeee!"

Middle-school guy humor. Gotta love it. Wait, another story idea. Guy humor vs. girl humor . . .

Not exactly page-one stuff. Nah.

But while I laughed with Troy and Andy, I worried about my own problem. I needed serious brainwork if I was going to work out a story.

Which meant that there was only one totally useless class I could cut in order to work on my ideas . . . that is, my *lack* of ideas.

Does anyone ever regret the gym classes they missed? Get real.

◆◆◆

Coach Tickner struggled with the combination lock on my gym locker. "Are you sure it's ten-sixteen-thirty-one?" she asked.

"Positive," I said. "I don't know why it won't work all of a sudden."

"Let me try again."

I watched Coach Tickner spin the tumbler. Of course it wouldn't work. I'd made up the combination of numbers. I would have felt guilty about making Coach Tickner wrestle with the lock, but I knew how much she loved wrestling.

Could I be on to another story here? How to scam a teacher. I could interview students about their best scam to get out of class. . . .

Double nah. Why reveal our secrets to the enemy?

"Must be broken." With a sigh the coach let the lock crash back against the locker.

"Gosh," I said. "I can't get to my gym uniform. I guess I can't participate." I tried to look properly disappointed. "Guess I'll just head off to study hall—"

"Whoa. Slow down, pardner." The coach gave me a keen look. Coach Tickner was a petite blonde who was way smarter than someone with sit-ups on the brain had any right to be. "I just got a new shipment of uniforms in. You can borrow one. You're wearing sneakers, and I can loan you a pair of socks. I keep a supply in my office."

"Fantastic." I gulped. "Lucky me."

"Thought you'd be pleased." Coach Tickner grinned. "Now follow me."

I trudged after her reluctantly.

She pushed open the door to her office, which consisted of one battered metal desk and a whole lot of athletic equipment. She crossed over to the connecting Equipment Room door. It let out a loud *squeeeeaaaak* as she opened it, like a chipmunk being strangled. She held it open with one hand while she scanned the shelves crammed with athletic equipment.

"They must be in the supply closet," she murmured. She said over her shoulder, "There's a fresh pair of socks in my desk drawer. Help yourself. I'll be back in a jiff." The Equipment Room door closed behind her with another dying chipmunk *squeeeeak*. It didn't shut all the way, and a second later, I heard the *whoosh* of the other door of the Equipment Room as the coach stepped out into the hall.

Great. Fantastic. Here I was, surrounded by coach-type things like balls and whistles, and I could be sitting at a computer in the *Real News* office. I wondered what would happen if I just left.

Before I could even think about getting up, though, I heard the *whoosh* of the Equipment Room door again, the one that led to the hallway. The coach was back already, and I hadn't even changed my socks.

Then I heard voices. It was not the coach. Most definitely not.

"But I—" a girl started saying.

"Shhhh," a boy warned. "You want to wake up the whole school? Everyone's out on the soccer field, but I don't want to take any chances."

The girl said something I couldn't make out. I eased myself out of my seat and crept toward the door. I'm drawn to a story the way a little kid is drawn to a puddle. When we find them, we both have to jump in. Of course, that's the trouble with puddles. You never know how deep they are until you step in them.

"Look," the girl whispered. "I paid good money. What's the holdup? The test is Friday!"

I eased closer to the door and put my eye to the crack. Whoever was there was outside of my range of vision. But if I opened the door any wider, it would let out that *squeeeeaaak*.

"Just do what I tell you," the boy said in an urgent voice. "I'm not taking any chances. Leave your backpack in the Student Activities Room five minutes before the fourth-period bell. Third cubbyhole down from the top, in the row closest to the door. Got that?"

"Got it. But—"

"Will you chill? Nobody will notice. You're in there all the time, anyway. Come back in fifteen minutes, and it'll be in your pack."

"But how will I get out of class?"

"That's your problem."

In the Student Activities Room, there was a shelving unit made up of cubicles for students to stow backpacks and books while they met there for clubs or activities. I strained closer to the door. What exactly was the guy going to leave in her backpack?

"Look, relax," the boy said. "I've done this five times already."

"You're sure it's the answer key?"

"You'll ace the test, okay?" The boy sounded impatient.

"You'll ace the test." "Answer key." The boy was selling answers! What a weasel! But how did he get them? This smelled worse than the cafeteria dumpster on a hot day.

"I'm out of here," Weasel Boy muttered.

I heard movement and the *whoosh* of the door.

I sprang forward and put my eye against the crack. Weasel Boy was already gone, so I didn't see him. All I could see of the girl was part of her leg as she left. She was wearing lime-green socks.

The culprits were gone. But I had my front-page scoop.

Reporter Goes Undercover—Under Table!

OKAY, SO I ONLY had part of a scoop. But I had some clues. I could put the pieces together. While I sat on the bench as a soccer alternate, I scribbled everything I knew in my notebook before I forgot the details.

Test is on Friday. Could be Lanigan's sixth-grade math??? Find out what other big tests are on Friday. . . . HOW?
Boy gave test to FIVE other students.
A cheating ring??? One of the buyers is wearing LIME-GREEN SOCKS.
Drop-off: Student Activities Room. Five

minutes before fourth period bell.

Five minutes before my lunch period ends.

Row closest to the door.

Third cubbyhole down from the top.

Obviously, I had my work cut out for me: First, check out every girl's ankles. After that: Stakeout!

I ducked under the table in the cafeteria for the fourth time.

GIRL REPORTER TOO EMBARRASSED TO SHOW HER FACE IN LUNCHROOM!

I must have looked pretty ridiculous with my head hanging around my knees. But I'd already tried cruising around the room, looking down at everyone's feet. I had to stop when I bumped into Kevin Sharpe and spilled his tray of food down his shirt. Chili on plaid flannel is not pretty.

My gaze scanned the sea of legs. I saw running shoes, hiking boots, clogs and one pair of Birkenstocks with purple socks. That was Ringo, who was sitting at my table.

But I didn't see a pair of lime-green socks. Lime-green socks that were loud enough to jump up and shout: GUILTY!

Suddenly, Ringo's head ducked underneath the table. "Whoa, coolness," he said, gazing around the cafeteria. "I always wondered what the world would look like sideways."

I sighed. "You *already* look at the world sideways."

We both straightened up. I returned my attention to my plate of tasteless tubes with orange glue, otherwise known as mac and cheese.

"So, wassup?" Ringo said, digging into his yogurt. "You've been on another planet since we sat down."

"I'm working on a hot lead," I said.

"Well, you said you'd have something by lunchtime," Ringo said. "Toni said no way, but I banked on it."

"Toni said no way?" I asked, my fork in the air.

Ringo nodded. "She lacks faith in general. I wouldn't take it personally."

But I did. I sort of liked Toni. She had talent and guts and almost as much ambition as I did. Plus a little boom-chicka-boom—an extra push to her personality that made her stand out in a crowd. My grandmother, who is also a journalist, says that boom-chicka-boom is a gift. Either you got it, or you don't. My gram has it. I like to think I do too.

But back to Ringo. "So, where's Megan?" I asked

him, spearing a macaroni. I wasn't ready to spill my complete story idea, but I wanted to give her a fat, juicy hint that I was on to another scoop. In fact, I couldn't wait.

"She's studying through lunch," Ringo told me. "She's got some majorly hard math test coming up." He pushed aside his empty yogurt and began to doodle on a napkin.

"Me, too. Don't remind me." Oops! I suddenly remembered that I'd promised to drop my homework in Mr. Lanigan's box by lunchtime. Well, I'd just have to do it after the stakeout. Scoops rate over teachers, even Terminators.

"She's freaked," Ringo said, drawing Simon peering under a table. "Math's her worst subject. And she's the straight-A type. Compulsive."

Which was why I had to impress her by delivering the scoop I'd promised. I dived under the table again and scanned student legs.

"What are we looking for, Casey?" Ringo asked from above. "Clue me in."

"Yeah, clue us in, Casey." That from a pair of top-of-the-line athletic shoes, the clunky kind with gels and pumps and swooshes. "Are you doing an exposé on how clean the cafeteria floor is?"

I straightened and saw Gary's smirk. "I'm doing a feature on how jocks are into the stupidest sneakers," I said. "Are you available for a photo op?"

"Yukkety yuk," Gary said, plunking down his tray.

"Gary!" Ringo exclaimed. "I was just thinking about you. Is that weird, or what? Like I summoned you with my mind."

"Either that or the fact that Gary has lunch this period," I muttered.

"The universe is full of weird patterns like that," Ringo said, dropping his pen. "Big balls of matter, revolving around other big balls. Circling in orbits. *Patterned* orbits. Constantly in motion. But going to the same place. Constantly—"

"Earth to Ringo," Gary said.

"Which reminds me," Ringo said, turning to Gary. "Speeding balls—sports. Not my thing. Which is why you put me down in the meeting this morning?"

Cautiously, I sipped my Snapple. I found I was following Ringo's logic. Very scary.

"No offense," Gary said, taking a bite of his sandwich. "Everyone can't be me, I guess."

"No, I'm *glad* you did it," Ringo said. I put my Snapple down. I had *no* idea what was coming next. That's one reason I like Ringo. "You made me realize that I have this huge gap in my education. Sure, I'm a Frisbee freak. But I guess that doesn't qualify as a sport."

"Frisbee is a way to pass the time, buddy,"

Gary said, chewing. "Not a sport."

"Cool, okay. I mean, who am I to argue with a sportswriter, right? So I've decided to take up a real sport," Ringo announced, beaming. I gagged on my mac and cheese.

"Great!" Gary approved. He flashed his confident, perfect smile to Ringo, and kicked me under the table. "So, which one? Soccer? Basketball? Baseball?"

"Cheerleading," Ringo said proudly.

I dropped my fork.

Gary gaped at Ringo. Luckily, he had already swallowed his bite of ham sandwich, so we were spared anything truly gross.

"Wish me luck," Ringo said cheerfully. "Tryouts are on Friday after school."

"Did you buy your little skirt yet?" Gary asked witheringly.

Go! Fight! Win! . . . Hey!

Ringo shook his head. "No, but I do have a rad pair of jams."

"Ringo, hold on," I said. I had to nip this little idea in the bud. "Didn't I ever tell you about my cheerleader theory? They're smack in the Barf Zone."

"The Barf Zone?" Ringo asked, puzzled.

"You got it. Along with the Spice Girls and rutabagas."

Ringo looked alarmed. "Not rutabagas!"

"Cheerleaders are an *accessory*," I continued, warming to my theme. "Like a purse. You can get along just fine in life without one. Cheerleaders are *decoration*. Think of them as tinsel."

Ringo frowned. I felt I was getting through. Until he opened his mouth.

"Okay, tell me this. What kind of zone do you have for cheerleaders who *eat* rutabagas?"

"Ringo, listen up, man," Gary broke in before I could respond. "You can't do this to me. I'm actually starting to like you, and I can't associate with a guy cheerleader. So before you make a decision, let me help you. What do you say?"

"What are you talking about, Gary?" I asked warily. I was glad Gary was as opposed to this cheerleader insanity as I was, but I had the sneaking suspicion it wasn't for the same reasons.

"I'm going to give Ringo guy lessons," Gary

said. "I'll teach him all about guy sports. We'll do one a day until Friday. Then you'll pick the one you like best. How does that sound?"

"You'd do that for me?" Ringo asked. "Whoa, coolness, Gary."

"Hit the pause button," I said. We were going from bad to equally bad. "Ringo, I'm totally opposed to the cheerleader idea. But that doesn't mean you have to let Gary turn you into one of those jock clones he hangs with."

"Cloning is awesome," Ringo said. "Don't you think that Dolly sheep is cute?"

"Ringo, focus," I said. "You're just not a macho guy. And that's *good.*"

"If he wants to learn, why not let him?" Gary challenged me.

"Because I know you," I told him. "You'll have him slapping guys on the butt and saying, 'How 'bout them Bulls?' like a complete moron."

"Not bulls, Casey," Ringo said. "Sheep. We haven't cloned a bull yet. Which is fine, because sheep are so much less violent."

Gary rolled his eyes. "Can't you see the guy needs help? He's got to get along in Guy World, Casey. I mean, in case you haven't noticed, Ms. Ace Reporter, he's a guy."

I jumped up. It wasn't like me to drop out in the middle of an argument, but I'd just caught a glimpse of the clock. I only had five minutes to get to the Activities Room for the stakeout. I had to see who put her backpack in the cubby. Then I had to see who slipped the answer key into the backpack. I would be incredibly late for my fifth-period class, but I'd think of some kind of excuse, like bad macaroni. Anyone who'd eaten in our school cafeteria would believe that.

"Hold that thought," I said. "Gotta go. I'll catch you guys later."

I sped off. I didn't feel comfortable leaving Ringo under Gary's influence, but I had more important fish sticks to fry.

I dashed down the hall and up the back stairs. Just as I skidded around a corner, I almost bumped into a teacher. Mr. Lanigan. The Terminator. Uh-oh.

"Ah, Ms. Smith," Mr. Lanigan said. "Funny I should run into you. I just came from my mailbox, which was strangely empty."

"That's because I was on my way to my locker right now to get my homework," I said, trying to sound perky. Okay, perky is a stretch for me. But I tried. "I had to eat first, Mr. Lanigan. I have this blood sugar thing. If I don't eat lunch, I faint. Crash, boom, Casey on the floor."

Mr. Lanigan didn't look too sympathetic. He's just about the most buttoned-up button-down teacher we have here at Trumbull. He's always in a white shirt and a tie that looks like it's strangling him. Tell me this: If men run the world, why don't they stop wearing neckties? How smart is it to start every day by tying a little noose around your neck?

"The homework you owe me is in your locker?" he asked dryly.

"Absolutely," I said. "Let me get it right now and bring it to you." I had to get away from him. I had barely two minutes to get to the Student Activities Room.

"Good," he said. "I'll go with you."

"You'll what?" I gulped.

"Come on, Casey," he said, starting to walk. "Where's your locker?"

Now I was really stuck. I knew I couldn't talk my way around Terminator Lanigan. But I couldn't lose the chance to find out who was buying test answers. It was my big story!

"Mr. Lanigan?" I hurried to keep up with his long stride. "I just remembered something. My homework is in my backpack. Which is in the Student Activities Room."

He raised an eyebrow at me. "You just remembered. How curious. But fine. We'll go there."

At least now we were heading in the right direction. Except, of course, that when we got there, we wouldn't find my homework. But I'd figure something out by then. I hoped.

We reached the Student Activities Room, and I peeked through the window before opening the door. The room was empty.

"Let's move it, Casey," Mr. Lanigan said. "The bell is about to ring."

We went inside. I crossed to the third cubby down from the top. There was a backpack already inside. I'd missed Lime-Green Sock Girl. But what about Weasel Boy?

"This looks like mine," I babbled. "Let me make sure—"

I yanked it out. It was unzipped, and books and papers spilled out. One paper wafted on a draft and landed at Mr. Lanigan's feet. He picked it up.

"Is this your homework?" he asked, reading it. "It doesn't look—"

He stopped. His eyes narrowed. His fingers suddenly clenched the paper. Then his flinty gaze moved to me.

"I'd like an explanation," he said. "This is the answer key to the math test I'm giving on Friday. And it was in *your* backpack."

This situation was out of control. But then I realized I could cover my butt *and* find out who the girl was. "It isn't my backpack, Mr. Lanigan!" I said. "I swear! I'll prove it!" I bent down and picked up a notebook that had fallen out of the knapsack. Written on the front in clear block letters with little glitter sparkles surrounding it was a name. It said:

Megan O'Connor

Dirt Between Floor Tiles Holds New Appeal

MY FINGERS TIGHTENED around the notebook. I don't know how they knew to do that, since my brain had come to a full stop. Megan was Lime-Green Sock Girl? Megan the Super?

"Casey? Let me see that," Mr. Lanigan said sternly.

"No way." I whipped the notebook behind my back. "I mean, it's nothing. Just a notebook. Nothing . . ."

He shot a lethal look at me. Who did I think I was, defying the Terminator? He held out his hand, saying nothing.

Slowly I handed it to him. His lips tightened when he read the name.

"Mr. Lanigan," I croaked. "I'm sure that—"

"Come along, Casey." Mr. Lanigan grabbed Megan's backpack and waited until I gathered the stuff on the floor and went ahead of him out the door.

I knew exactly where we were going—the principal's office. And though Ms. Nachman could be soft and fuzzy, I knew she would draw the line at cheating.

GIRL REPORTER FOUND TO BE
CHEATER-CHEATER PUMPKIN-EATER!
Never meant to do any harm, she cries.

While we marched, my brain clicked into overdrive. What had Megan's backpack been doing in the third cubby? Had it been Megan in the Equipment Room before? Wouldn't I have recognized her voice? No, I wouldn't. The girl had spoken almost in a whisper. It had been hard to pick up any words at all.

But Megan *couldn't* have bought an answer key. She was so honest and straightforward. She was a straight-A student and a hard worker. She didn't need to cheat.

Then Ringo's words floated into my brain.

"She's freaked. Math's her worst subject. And she's the straight-A type. Compulsive."

And hadn't Weasel Boy said that the buyer of the answers was in the Student Activities Room "all the time?" Megan was on the Yearbook Committee. It met in the Activities Room.

As we walked down the empty halls toward the Office of Doom, I frantically tried to remember what color Megan's socks had been this morning. But until this particular episode came along, I hadn't paid much attention to footwear.

"Couldn't we talk about this first, Mr. Lanigan?" I asked. "I just know that Megan is innocent. She would never cheat."

Mr. Lanigan sighed. The grim line of his mouth relaxed a little. "Casey, kids do surprising things when they're under pressure. Even good kids."

"What's going to happen?" I asked.

"First of all, you're going to explain exactly what you were doing in that room," Mr. Lanigan said. "I have a feeling that you know more than you're saying. And second, we're going to hear from Megan."

I knew what that meant. Megan's name would be boomed over the P.A. system.

"MEGAN O'CONNOR TO THE PRINCIPAL'S OFFICE IMMEDIATELY!"

Everyone would hear it. Already, Megan would sound guilty of something. And then, when she got to the principal's office, who would she find there?

Me. Megan would think that I turned her in!

I'd only seen Ms. Nachman at assemblies, when she was up on a stage and I was sitting in about the fiftieth row, way over on the side. She always seemed nice. She even cracked a few jokes that were actually funny. But sitting face-to-face with her across a desk was seriously scary.

Even though I knew I wasn't the cheater, I still felt guilty. Even my *socks* were sweating. There was something about that big mahogany desk and her leather chair and that brass lamp that all screamed, "Liar, liar, pants on fire!"

While we waited for Megan, I babbled out the whole story.

"You and Megan work together on *Real News*," Ms. Nachman said. "Do you think you would have recognized her voice?"

I wanted to say yes. I wanted to say, "Of course I'd recognize Megan's voice, and it wasn't hers." But I couldn't.

I shook my head again. "I really couldn't tell," I admitted.

GIRL REPORTER FAILS TO PROTECT PAL

There was a knock at the door. "Come in," Ms. Nachman said.

Megan walked in. She was wearing her gym uniform. She saw me and raised her eyebrows in a question. I immediately looked at her feet. She was wearing white socks, but that was because she was in her gym uniform. I hated the fact that I had to check out Megan's socks, but I couldn't help it. A good reporter goes on facts, not feelings.

Ms. Nachman held up the answer key. "What can you tell us about this, Megan?"

Megan looked puzzled. "What is it?"

"It's an answer key to Mr. Lanigan's test on Friday," Ms. Nachman said. "Can you tell us what it was doing in your backpack?"

Megan just stared for a moment. Then her face flushed. "I-I don't know what you're talking about."

She almost looked . . . well, guilty. Why? Or maybe she was surprised and scared?

"Casey overheard an exchange in which one student bought the answer key from another student," Ms. Nachman said. "This student was supposed to leave her backpack in a certain cubby at a certain time. Casey found your backpack in the prearranged location."

Megan flashed a look of disbelief at me. I wanted to crawl between the floor tiles. Ms.

Nachman made it sound as though I'd tried to trap Megan!

"I left my backpack there because I was helping Ms. Woodham carry art supplies," Megan said. Her voice shook a little bit. "She stopped me in the hall, and I just dropped it off to help her to the art room. I was going to run back and get it, but the bell rang, and I didn't want to be late for gym."

"Then what was the test doing in your pack, Megan?" Mr. Lanigan said.

"I don't know," Megan said.

"Who sold you the test, Megan?" Ms. Nachman asked softly.

"I'm telling you, I'm innocent!" Megan exclaimed. One tear snaked down her cheek.

Ms. Nachman sighed. "I don't know what to think, Megan. The evidence is not in your favor." She paused, looking sadly at Megan, and then continued, "The matter must be put before the Honor Council when it meets on Friday. Until then, I'm going to have to suspend you from all extracurricular activities."

Megan's chin lifted. Tears stood in her eyes. "I guess you have to do that."

"Does that include *Real News*?" I blurted out.

"That includes everything," Ms. Nachman said.

Megan didn't look at me. I saw her swallow painfully, as though she had a sore throat. "Can I go now, Ms. Nachman?"

The principal nodded. Megan almost ran out the door.

We all watched her go. I wondered if the other two felt as wormlike as I did. I wanted to run after her. I wanted to shout, "Megan, I didn't turn you in! I know you're innocent."

But I *didn't* know if she was innocent. I *wanted* to think so. I *believed* she was, but I didn't *know.*

I turned back to Ms. Nachman and Mr. Lanigan. "Can I ask a favor? Can you please, please not do anything yet? I'm an investigative reporter. Let me investigate! I think I have a couple of clues. If you could just let me do some digging, maybe I can come up with who sold the test and who bought it."

"Oh, Casey," Ms. Nachman murmured. "I don't know—"

"Ms. Nachman, Megan O'Connor is a good student," I interrupted. Extreme times call for extreme measures. "If she says she's innocent, shouldn't you give her the benefit of the doubt? You don't want to trash her reputation without the facts."

"I wouldn't do that, Casey," Ms. Nachman said. "What I'm hoping is that if we announce that we have the answer key, the seller will come forward."

"Dream on," I snorted.

Ms. Nachman frowned, and I realized I'd been rude—to the principal. Oops—rewind! "I'm sorry," I said quickly. "I just know kids. This is someone who has no problem stealing and selling answers, and getting others to cheat. He sure isn't going to step forward. This kid sounded cocky."

That was true. The kid hadn't sounded scared, or nervous. He was a cool customer.

"Look, the test is on Friday, Will you give me until then? Please?" I didn't mention that the *Real News* deadline was on Friday too, and that I hoped to clear Megan and have my scoop in one fell blow. No need to confuse them. I looked at the principal, then Mr. Lanigan. "Mr. Lanigan can give a different test. That way, if anyone bought the answers, they'll be in big trouble anyway."

Ms. Nachman and Mr. Lanigan exchanged glances.

"All right," Ms. Nachman said. "We don't want rumors to get around the school before the Honor Council meets. So you have until Friday morning. We won't announce to the students that we know the test is out there, and we'll have Mr. Lanigan give out a new test."

"Thank you." I smiled. "And it'll give me time to clear Megan."

"Three days." Ms. Nachman held up three fingers. "That's it, Casey. And if the evidence points to Megan, you have to tell us. We need to give the Honor Council all the facts. Got that?"

It wasn't really three days. It was more like two and a half. I only had the rest of Tuesday, Wednesday, and Thursday to uncover the facts. But I wasn't about to quibble.

"Got it. Thank you again, Ms. Nachman," I said fervently. Then I ran out after Megan.

I found Megan at her locker. She was slipping her denim jacket over her gym uniform. It was the first time I'd seen her wear things that didn't match.

"Are you leaving?" I asked. "But you don't have a pass."

"Oh, no. Does that mean I'll get in *trouble*?" Megan asked sarcastically.

Now, sarcasm was totally not Megan. And she wasn't the type to leave school without a pass. She was mucho-maximum upset. With reason. I didn't say anything. I didn't really know what to say.

Stiffly, Megan buttoned her jacket. "I thought we were getting along, Casey. I mean, we got out the first issue of *Real News* without killing each other."

"Megan, I didn't turn you in," I blurted out. "I mean, I sort of did, but I didn't know it was you at the time. It was just that I didn't turn in my math homework, and the paper flew out, and—"

"Save it." Megan's voice was clipped. "Everything's a joke or a story to you, right? Well, ha, ha. You got me good this time. Both ways."

Okay, now I felt like the *dirt* in the crack *between* the floor tiles. "Megan—"

"Do you have what you want now?" Megan asked, her face red. "You can write about whatever you want. You don't have to listen to me anymore."

"But I don't want—" I shook my head. I hadn't even thought that part through. How were we going to make our Friday deadline without Megan? How could there be a new issue of *Real News* without its editor?

"What was the first question you asked when Ms. Nachman suspended me from school activities?" Megan challenged. Her voice changed, as if she were mimicking me. "'Does that include *Real News*, Ms. Nachman?' Well, it does! And isn't it all a big, huge joke? Ha, ha, Casey! I think I'll just about die laughing!"

"Megan—"

But I couldn't finish the sentence. Megan rushed off, stumbling toward the stairs.

Girl Reporter Has No Clue

I THOUGHT I'D had a huge scoop. Instead, I'd gotten Megan in trouble. I scribbled in my journal.

Megan is . . .

A.) innocent and wrongly accused

OR

B.) guilty and very messed up.

Neither scenario was funny at all.

I was late for Spanish with Mr. Roney, but he only gave me a severe look as I slipped into my seat. I took out my journal. I didn't have a minute to waste. And Mr. Drone-y wasn't exactly the most fascinating speaker—in *any* language.

I had to start now if I wanted to investigate the cheating ring. If what I found out cleared Megan, great. If she was guilty, I'd find that out too. But I couldn't ignore the truth.

I turned to a blank page in my journal.

Who Bought the Test?

A girl who:

- Wears lime-green socks
- Uses the Student Activities Room a lot
- Is in one of Mr. Lanigan's sixth-grade classes

Who Sold It???

A Boy

Not much to go on.

But wait a second. I had forgotten the most important question of all.

??????? PLUS, HOW DID SOMEONE STEAL THE ANSWER KEY FROM MR. LANIGAN IN THE FIRST PLACE????

And I had to find out the answers to all these questions by Friday. I needed:

HEEEEELP!

After class I had a free period. I still hadn't dropped off my homework in Mr. Lanigan's box. First things first, though. I headed for the pay phones, dropped in a quarter and called home.

My concept of "home" may be looser than most. My parents are both doctors, and they're involved in this group called Doctors Without Borders. They fly all over the world, anywhere doctors are needed. Right now they're in Southeast Asia, helping the local population after a huge chemical spill. Tackling problems runs in my family.

My sixteen-year-old brother, Billy, went with my parents. He said he went for the "cultural experience." My parents said they didn't really feel comfortable leaving him here. His grades at Abbington High were in the basement, and they wanted him close by so they could hound him.

I said great. This way I got to have my grandmother all to myself.

Now, I bet you're thinking living with a grandmother would be some kind of cozy, cookie-baking experience, right?

Wrong. Gram isn't *cozy.* She's a full-throttle experience. She's a famous journalist who's been on TV, written books and published stories in major magazines and newspapers. For years. She has a townhouse in New York filled with her awards and her books and photos of the really smart people she entertains. And she left it all behind—for *me.*

Gram says that a few months of quiet isolation are just what she needs to focus on her current project. She's putting down all of her experiences in a book. She might be getting a little silvery gray in her red-blond hair, but she's still full of boom-chicka-boom. In fact, that's where I got mine.

I had to let the phone ring about ten times before Gram picked up. This didn't surprise me. I knew she was working, and when she is, she concentrates really hard.

"Hey, Gram," I said. "Favor." I don't waste words with my gram. I don't need to.

"Shoot."

"Can we go underwear shopping another day? I'm on to a story here at school," I said.

"Oh, Casey. We keep postponing this shopping trip. One more washing and your undies are going to disintegrate into string art," Gram said distractedly. "What would your mother say?"

"She can't see me. Or my underwear. And I won't tell if you won't," I answered.

"Okay," Gram said, sounding a little relieved. "Actually, it would be better for me, too. I have a long way to go with this chapter. I've fallen in the middle of a paragraph and I can't get up. And I promised my editor I'd have these pages to him tomorrow."

I grinned, picturing Gram in her "deadline" outfit—a red silk dragon kimono thrown over a pair of leggings and a big T-shirt that blared RUNS WITH SCISSORS. When Gram is on deadline, personal appearance takes a major backseat.

"Thanks, Gram," I said.

"See you later, sweetie," Gram said. "You can tell me all about your story tonight. I haven't had a chance to go to the store, so it's going to be—"

"Takeout Chinese," I finished. "Awesome."

"Radical," she answered. Gram likes to tease me when I use slang by throwing it right back at me. "Slang superlatives," Gram calls it. She complains that I rely too much on the cliches of my generation. That's how Gram talks. But you can't help being crazy about her.

I still had time before my next class, so I headed toward the administration office. On my way I passed this little room that the guidance counselors use for conferences. It has these big comfy armchairs and a window overlooking the athletic fields. I caught a flash of someone curled up in an armchair, and I stopped. It was Megan.

I took a hesitant step inside. Megan glanced

up at me, then swished her head toward the window as if an alien spacecraft were landing in the soccer field. It had started to rain again, and it pattered against the thick panes of the window.

"I thought you were going home," I said.

"I just needed some air," she said. "And I didn't have a pass, remember? Don't worry, I'm not cutting a class. This is my free period."

Even in a time of crisis, Megan couldn't break the rules. Shouldn't that tell me something? Why couldn't I get rid of this tiny nagging doubt that she could be guilty?

"Megan, I'm really sorry about what happened," I blurted out, moving a little farther into the room. "Mr. Lanigan saw the test before I could do anything."

"Okay," Megan said softly. "But do you think I'm guilty?"

"Of course not," I said automatically. My voice didn't sound all that convincing to me, though.

Megan sighed. "I didn't know you were a liar, Casey," she said. I guess it didn't convince Megan either. "A pain in the neck, sure. But you always shoot from the hip."

I sat in the other armchair. Obviously, I couldn't skate my way around this situation. "Okay, here's the deal. Of course I *want* to think you're innocent, Megan. And it's hard for me to believe that anyone who eats exactly five servings of fruit and vegetables a day would cheat. But let's look at the facts. I don't know you that well yet. You're kind of compulsive about grades, and you're nervous about Lanigan's test. And the test *was* in your backpack."

I took a deep breath. "And remember what you told me last week during the factory pollution story? That I shouldn't let my own opinion sway me? That I had to look at the facts? Well, I think that's pretty good advice."

Megan was quiet for a second. "I guess you're right," she said slowly. "And that's what everybody in school is going to think, too. Everyone is going to wonder if I'm guilty."

"Not if we catch the bad guys," I said. Quickly I explained the deal I'd struck with Ms. Nachman.

"So, if I can figure out who's in the cheating ring by Friday, you'll be cleared," I finished.

And if I couldn't clear Megan? I wondered. What then? I could see the headline of *Real News*:

NEWSPAPER EDITOR INVOLVED IN CHEATING RING!

Megan would be suspended, or expelled. And who would take over as editor?

Stop, Casey. Don't go there. Just don't. You

wouldn't want the job under these circumstances, would you? *Would you?*

"But what about *now*?" Megan interrupted my dark fantasy. "People will know I'm in trouble. They'll think I did something wrong."

"Nobody knows," I insisted. "Nobody will know."

Megan bit her lip. "Though people will wonder why I'm suddenly not showing up for Yearbook. And Drama Club. And there's *Real News* to think about. Mr. Baxter wants to cancel the issue for next week. I told him what happened, and what the principal said."

"What?" I shrieked. "Is he crazy?"

"He said something about lack of editorial leadership. After all, I can't participate—"

"But you've already nailed down most of the articles!" I interrupted. "Sure, the issue isn't totally there yet. But we've got three whole days."

Megan winced. "Which was exactly his point. Not much time."

"Shouldn't we all decide that?" I asked hotly.

Megan shrugged. "It isn't my decision anymore, Casey," she said faintly. "I'm out for the duration, remember?"

"I'll talk to Mr. Baxter," I told Megan. No paper—so much for my scoop! I had to jump in and stop this madness. "He's got to have more faith in us. In the meantime let's focus on uncovering this cheating ring. Before the Honor Council meets on Friday."

"That doesn't give us much time," Megan said. "What do we have to go on?"

I summarized the meeting I'd overheard, and Megan fired questions at me. Was there anything distinguishing about their voices? Did they mention if they were cutting a class? Did they sound as though they were friends?

All good questions. Too bad my answers were mostly "I don't know."

"So . . . we're looking for a boy," Megan said, frowning. "And a girl with green socks."

"That's about as far as I've gotten," I said.

"But you're a good reporter," Megan said. "The thing to do is figure out your next step. I suggest cross-checking the names on Mr. Lanigan's class rosters against the students who meet in the Activities Room."

"Bor-ing!" I said, disappointed. I didn't want to compare names—I wanted to take action!

"Sometimes the boring stuff gets results," Megan said. "Do you have a better idea?"

Okay, I didn't. But I seriously hated it when Megan thought of something before I did. "I'll call in the troops to help," I said, admitting defeat.

"I know the Yearbook Committee meets in

the Activities Room," Megan mused. "And the Student Council does, too. I'm not sure who else, but there's a schedule posted right inside the door. You should check that first."

"Yes, sir," I said. Since when had Megan taken charge of the investigation?

"I have a list of all club members on the PC in the *Real News* office. Just look under the school clubs file," Megan continued, ignoring my tone. She often ignored it. That might be why we hadn't killed each other. Yet.

"You have a list?" I asked, dumbfounded. It would save me time, but I couldn't believe Megan had gone to all that trouble.

She shrugged. "I did it the first week, when we were deciding what to do with the paper. I thought it might come in handy. We'll be doing a lot of articles on school clubs."

"You've got to get a life," I said. Megan was so organized she was *pre*organized. Did she ever sleep? Or relax?

Megan turned her face to the window again. "You'd better get started," she said. "Let me know if you need me."

I stood up and walked across the room. I hesitated by the door. "Megan, I'm really sorry," I said.

"Yeah, I know. Thanks for trying to help me,

Casey." Megan's voice drifted over to me, so low I had to strain to hear her. "But you know what? I just wish you'd believed I was innocent. Not because of facts. But because we're friends."

It wasn't often that Megan O'Connor could shut me up. But at that moment I stood there, gaping like a fish in an aquarium. I didn't know what to say.

So I left.

Great Minds Baffled by Impossible Theft

I GRABBED MY math homework from my locker and slipped it into Mr. Lanigan's box. Finally.

Then I checked out his schedule. He had a free period, too. He was monitoring the Math Resource Center. I hustled up to the third floor.

Mr. Lanigan was correcting papers at the front desk while three students huddled over a computer, working out a problem.

Quickly, I outlined what I needed. He nodded.

"Sure, I can give you class rosters. I'll print them out." Mr. Lanigan picked up his laptop and crossed to the printer. He accessed a file and clicked, and a moment later pages began to roll out of the printer. "By the way, I hope your homework is in my box as we speak," he said.

"It is," I said. Then I asked, "Mr. Lanigan, do

you have any idea how the answer key got stolen?"

"I've been thinking about that one too," Mr. Lanigan said with a frown. "I have to say I'm stumped. I worked on the test right here in the Resource Center, the way I usually do. Then I printed my copy out—the one with the answers—on this printer."

"Hold on," I said, going over to a PC. "You wrote up the test on one of these computers? Maybe somebody copied the file off the hard drive."

He shook his head. "I always delete that file," he said, "in order to prevent just that. Then I locked the hard copy and my laptop in my briefcase. And I always keep the case with me—in case you were going to ask about that."

I wasn't. I didn't need to. The briefcase is definitely part of Mr. Lanigan's FBI profile.

"What about the keys?" I asked.

"I keep them in my jacket pocket." He reached into the interior chest pocket of his tweed sport coat and withdrew the keys. "So I'm baffled."

I was, too. How could someone get the keys, then get into his briefcase, without his noticing? It seemed impossible. Mr. Lanigan never took off his jacket. He wasn't a dress-down Friday kind of guy. Could the thief be an expert pickpocket?

Even for me, that idea seemed totally farfetched.

I took the list of class rosters, and Mr. Lanigan gave me a hall pass so that I wouldn't be snagged by a teacher. I still had a free period, but we weren't supposed to roam the halls. And I'd really been pushing my luck.

I made my way through the empty halls to the Student Activities Room. There I looked at the bulletin board to see which clubs met regularly in the room. Then I copied down those clubs in my journal:

Debating Squad

Yearbook Committee

Student Council

But since Student Council elections weren't for another two weeks, the council from last year had only met once since school started. I knew that because I was planning to write the "What's Up with Our SC?" column for *Real News*. That left Debating Squad and Yearbook.

I still had a little time before the bell, so I hotfooted it to the *Real News* office. No one was there, so I turned on a computer and whipped up an e-mail for Griffin. He was my best friend through grade school. Actually, he's still my best friend, even though now he lives a few hundred miles away, in Baltimore.

TO: Thebeast
FROM: Wordpainter
RE: whatta day

First, I gave him the straight facts about my not-so-average morning. Then I added:

Megan has been accused (wrongly) . . . (I think). I'm going to nail the real losers—and clear Megan's name!

Okay—flip side. What if I fail? Or what if Megan * is * guilty? Would it be the end of the world? Would it be so awful if I had to be editor of *Real News*? Maybe I'm pond scum for even thinking that thought. But can I help the thoughts that pop into my head?

I was sending the e-mail off to Griffin when Toni burst in and swung her button-cluttered backpack onto the table at Dalmatian Station.

Great. Out of everyone on the staff, it had to be Toni. I could trash the idea of getting her help to clear Megan. When it came to Getting Along With Others, Toni rated a big fat F. Or at least a big fat "Incomplete."

"Listen up. We've got problems," I said.

Toni didn't look up from her photographs. "*We* got problems? I don't think so. If I had a problem, I'd know about it."

Terrific. I was off to a good start. I drew up one of the plastic chairs and sat next to her. "Toni, it's Megan."

She looked up. Her amber eyes were immediately concerned. "Megan?"

"She's in trouble." Quickly I outlined the situation.

Toni blew out a long breath. "Serious stuff. Can you imagine *anyone* thinking Megan O'Connor, the world's most perfect person, would cheat? Even Have-No-Mercy Nachman. Okay, girl, count me in."

Wow. I was surprised. No. On second thought, I wasn't. Toni talks tough, but I know she's a Megan fan. Now, if it had been *me* who was in trouble, I'd be swinging in a cold breeze right now.

I pushed the class roster toward her. "Megan has a list of Debating Squad and Yearbook members on the PC here. We have to cross-check it against Lanigan's class rosters and see which students show up on both lists."

"What are we waiting for?" Toni turned to the

PC. She pointed and clicked, searching Megan's files. "Here we go. I'll highlight the names of all the girls in the two clubs and print them out."

After the printer rolled out the names, Toni and I compared them together. We came up with the names of four girls who had Lanigan for Math, and also spent a lot of time in the Activities Room. They were:

```
Jessica Rundel, Debating Squad,
  Yearbook
Phoebe Trippett, Debating Squad
Natalie Klein, Yearbook
Angela Boltanski, Debating Squad
```

"Not exactly thief types," Toni said, running a short blue fingernail along the names. "I know Angela. She's completely cool. And it can't be Phoebe. She's so . . . straight-up and straight-A. Plus, she's a friend of Megan's. She wouldn't let Megan take the fall."

"I hear you. I met her this morning," I agreed. "But remember, no one knows *why* Megan's in trouble. And Jessica Rundel is her friend, too. She's not so straight-up, though. She's a straight-A jerk."

Toni grinned. "I'm not arguing, girl, but that doesn't make her a cheater."

"Well, I've got one piece of luck," I said. "The Debating Squad meets today after school. I can check out all three of the girls—and their socks. I don't know what to do about Natalie, though—"

Just then, the bell rang. Toni and I exchanged frustrated glances.

"Hang on," Toni said. "I can do a word search, and see if she's in any other clubs. It'll just take a second."

Toni typed in the name. "Swimming!" she announced after a moment.

"Maybe she has practice after school," I said, thinking. "I know the team has a big meet on Saturday. Gary could pretend to do a sports story."

Toni nodded. "Gary said something about showing Ringo how to play b-ball after school."

"Great!" I said, smacking the table. "We could nail the guilty person by the end of the day!"

"I hope so, for Megan's sake." Toni shook her head, her curls bouncing with the movement. "You or me, we could handle this. We go our own way, you know? But not Megan. She really cares what other people think of her. It's like . . . everything to her."

I frowned. This was true, on all counts.

Toni elbowed me. "Never thought the two of us could have something in common, did you, *Ace*?"

"You're right," I said. "For once."

We glared at each other. What can I say? It was a bonding moment.

Toni picked up her backpack. "Listen, I've got to get to science. I'm already running on Chillmark's last nerve."

I trailed after Toni and headed to my English class. I felt a little funny after our talk. It had never entered Toni's mind for a second that Megan could be guilty. Why had it entered mine? Ringo had said that Toni lacked faith in general. Then why did she have such a never-ending supply when it came to Megan?

And why didn't I?

I hurried into English class. Maybe I could grab Mr. Baxter for a second before class began and tackle him about keeping our Friday deadline for *Real News*. I barreled through the door.

But something was wrong.

The room smelled of spice and flowers. Perfume.

And a thin, youngish, almost pretty woman with sweeping waves of blond hair down her back sat at his desk. Lady Godiva—with clothes.

Substitute. Uh-oh.

But Mr. Baxter had been at our meeting that morning. "Where's Mr. Baxter?" I demanded.

"He's out for the rest of the day." She smiled. "I'm Ms. Carlucci."

"Will he be back tomorrow?" I asked her.

"I think so," she said carefully.

Obviously, she didn't know. But she wasn't about to tell that to a measly student. Meanwhile, I'd promised Megan I'd try to square things with our faculty advisor. But now he was gone, too.

Ever have one of those days when you feel like a salmon swimming in a river of sludge?

Student Debate Puts Audience to Sleep

As soon as the last bell rang, I scooted down to the gym to tackle Gary about sussing out Natalie Klein. Gary and Ringo were on the court. Gary held a basketball out by the tips of his fingers.

"Gross, Ringo!" he cried. "You got the ball all wet!"

"You said 'Dribble.'"

"Heads up, guys," I said. "I need help."

Gary nodded. "We got the 411 from Toni."

"How's Megan doing?" Ringo asked.

"Okay, I guess," I said. "Can you guys do some

leg work?" I showed them the list. "I think one of these four girls is guilty."

"Not to mention that she owns one wicked pair of green socks," Ringo observed.

"I know Natalie Klein," Gary said. "She's the champion backstroke on the girls' team. Toni already told me to check her out at today's practice. I can head over after we finish."

"Head over *now*," I said impatiently. "This is way more important than you trying to turn Ringo into superjock."

"That's not what I'm doing!" Gary protested. "I just want him to know he has options."

"Whoa, time out!" Ringo interrupted. Then he paused. "Hey, Gary, did you hear that? I used a sports term. Where was I? Oh. Time. We don't have much to play with. If we're going to help Megan, we've got to find the real cheater before Friday, right?"

Gary and I nodded.

"So here's the deal. Casey, go check out the Debating Squad. Gary and I will handle Natalie."

Under pressure, even Ringo could get organized. "Try to catch her before she changes into her suit," I said. "You've got to get a look at her socks."

I headed off to the Student Activities Room. I was glad that Ringo and Gary had pitched in to help. Somehow we'd become a real newspaper staff. A team. We were pulling for each other. A lot of that was due to Megan, I knew. She had pushed and prodded and yanked us along until we worked together as a unit.

So you want the truth? What would *Real News* be without Megan? Dismal.

When I got to the Activities Room, Toni was standing outside the closed door.

She grinned when she saw my surprised expression. "You can't fly solo all the time, Ace," she said.

"What's going on in there?" I asked. "Did you talk to anyone yet?"

Toni shook her head. "The squad is in the middle of some kind of mock debate. We're going to have to wait until after the meeting."

"Great," I groaned. "The only thing worse than being *on* the Debating Squad has to be *listening to* the Debating Squad."

"The good news is that we're on the right track," Toni told me. "One of those girls is definitely guilty."

"How can you be so sure?" I asked.

Toni stepped away from the door. "Take a look."

I peeked through small window in the door. Phoebe and Jessica were standing at opposite lecterns. The other students sat in rows, watching them.

I tried to figure out what Toni was showing me, but I was distracted as Jessica tossed her auburn hair behind her shoulder. She gestured with one hand at Phoebe. You could tell she was trying to score a point off her.

Ooh! There was something about her smug expression that really bugged me. She was one of Megan's best friends, and I totally didn't get it. The girl was so full of hot air she could be a float in the Macy's Thanksgiving Day Parade. Megan could be annoying—really annoying—but she was sincerely annoying.

"Look at Jessica," I said. "What a fraud."

"That's Angela Boltanski in the front row. Last seat on the left," Toni murmured. "In the blue sweater."

Angela had oval-framed wire-rimmed glasses and short, curly blond hair. I saw her roll her eyes as Jessica made a point. Already, I liked her.

"What do you mean, we're on the right track?" I whispered. "How can you tell?"

"Check out their feet," Toni said.

Of course! My gaze darted from Phoebe to Jessica to Angela to . . . I gasped.

All the girls on the debating team were wearing lime-green socks!

School Plagued by Green-Sock Epidemic

"AM I SEEING THINGS?" I asked, rubbing my eyes.

"I'm seeing it, too," Toni said. "Totally whacked."

Toni and I waited until the mock debate ended and the discussion was over. Then Ms. Hinkel, the faculty advisor, blabbed for about ten minutes. I thought Angela Boltanski's eyes would roll back in her head. I was liking the girl more and more. I hoped she wasn't the guilty one.

Finally, the meeting was over.

"I'll take Phoebe," I said. "Why don't you tackle Angela, since you know her? Ask her what she was doing second period today."

Toni headed for Angela, and I made a beeline for the other side of the room.

Phoebe shoved a notebook in her backpack, then checked her watch. She got up hurriedly.

"Phoebe! Hey!" I moved toward her quickly. "It's Casey, remember?"

"Sure," Phoebe said. "What's up?"

"Megan was really impressed with the draft of your story," I told her. "She was looking for you second period this morning to tell you. Don't you have a free period then?"

Phoebe shook her head. "I have social studies with Mrs. Maroni."

Darn. That meant it couldn't have been Phoebe in the Equipment Room.

"Oh. She thought she saw you in the hall," I said, shrugging.

"It wasn't me," Phoebe said impatiently. "Look, I'm sorry, Casey. I have to meet my mom, okay? I've got ballet, and if I'm late, she'll freak. I'll catch Megan tomorrow."

"But I—" I wanted to ask Phoebe why all of the girls on the Debating Squad were wearing the same socks.

But Phoebe had caught sight of a tall, anxious-looking woman in a navy suit. She stood in the doorway, tapping her wristwatch.

"Phoebe!" the woman said crisply. "Ballet!"

Phoebe jerked up like a marionette. With a

quick "'Bye, Casey," she rushed out the door.

Whoa. It was like watching a circus act. *Clap, jump.*

Don't get me wrong—I'm not crazy about having parents half a world away. It's tough, even with e-mail and phone calls. But at least they never treat me like a trained seal.

Jessica was buttering up Ms. Hinkel, so I looked for Toni. She headed toward me, shaking her head.

"Angela is a no-go," Toni said. "She was in science lab second period. I just learned a zillion disgusting things about dissecting a frog. I think I'm going to lose my lunch."

"Did you ask about the socks?" I prompted. No point wasting time bemoaning one less suspect. Besides, it meant Angela was in the clear.

She nodded. "It's like a lucky charm. At their first match Angela wore those green socks, and she just squeaked by with enough points to win the debate. So now all the girls wear the same socks for meetings and matches."

I winced. "Lucky socks?"

"Don't knock it." Toni nodded knowingly. "I'm totally into charms and things. My grandmother in Mexico? She casts spells all the time. And let me tell you, her magic works."

"Magic? Maybe. Green socks?" I shot a look at Jessica's lime-green anklets.

Toni followed my glance and shrugged. "Okay, the socks are a stretch. And that shade of green never brought anybody luck."

"Hey!" I shouted, the significance of Toni's and my conversation suddenly hitting me. "That leaves Jessica. She has to be the guilty one! I knew it all the time!"

Toni eyed me curiously. "You did? How?"

I didn't think answering "Because I can't stand her" would earn me points in the Journalistic Objectivity department. Just then, I noticed Jessica Rundel heading out the door. "Heads up," I said. "Our chicken just flew the coop. I'll catch you later."

I hurried into the corridor as Jessica disappeared into the girls' room. Following her in, I found her at the sink, fluffing her hair.

Okay, time out. If there's one thing I don't get about my fellow girls, it's the hair-brushing thing.

Personally, I figure I'm way ahead if my hair doesn't stick up in back like a duck's. I accept the fact that when you have basic boring brown hair and basic boring brown eyes, there just isn't that much you can do to improve on Mother Nature.

Of course, I do have one amazing asset. The

most perfect set of ears. Pinkish white and beautifully formed, like a seashell. But very few people get to see them. I keep them hidden under my hair, sort of like a secret weapon. Only *I* know their power and perfection.

But back to the hair-brushing thing. Jessica Rundel has this layered auburn hair halfway down her back and hazel eyes, so she has something to work with. And she works it. To death.

"I don't mean to interrupt vanity time," I said as Jessica leaned into the mirror to study her face. "But do you have a minute?"

Jessica shot me a look in the mirror. Okay, maybe it wasn't the best approach to cozy up to a suspect. But Jessica Rundel made my teeth hurt. And the way she was glaring at me, I had a feeling I got on her nerves, too. Go figure.

"I'm not being vain, okay?" she said, returning her attention to her fascinating self. "I have a *rash*. I found out I'm allergic to something. All of a sudden."

I switched from sarcasm to sympathy. It usually got better results. "A rash? That sounds awful."

"It *is*," Jessica agreed, still scrutinizing her face in the mirror. "You have no idea how *hard* it is to figure out what it is, okay? I have to go to an allergist and get all these scratch tests. It's like, brutal."

"Mmmm," I said. I couldn't see one tiny bit of redness on Jessica's face. "I don't see anything."

"You sure?" she asked, relieved.

"Positive. Listen, Jessica, *Real News* is doing a story on the Debating Squad, and—"

"Tell me about it. I got my picture taken on the day the rash started." Jessica rolled her eyes. "That Toni girl is so incredibly rude. She wouldn't reschedule."

"Oh, sorry." Thinking fast, I formed a quick lie. "She was taking some makeup shots this morning second period. Weren't you there?"

"You're kidding me!" Jessica looked furious. "She didn't tell me!" Then she hesitated. "Oh. I wasn't here, anyway. I had an appointment with my allergist this morning. I didn't get back until, like, third period."

This was crazy. So far, all of my suspects had alibis! Either somebody was lying, or I was off base somehow. Unless Gary came through with Natalie Klein. But what were the chances of Natalie owning a hideous pair of socks, too?

"Casey." Jessica interrupted my thoughts. "Is that like, all? I'm kind of busy here."

"Oh, right." Apparently there were a few

hundred pores Jessica hadn't examined yet.

Backing toward the door, I added, "And I hope that rash gets better soon. I mean, you don't want to make a *rash* decision. Or a *rash* statement. Especially when you're on the debating team."

Jessica just rolled her eyes. What can I say? Some people have no sense of humor.

Studies Prove Takeout Increases Brain Cells

I RODE MY BIKE home through the wet streets of Abbington. The weather had been pretty warmish, but this rain had brought a hint of the icy winter to come. The shops on Main Street were empty, and the park was deserted. Nobody wanted to be out in this cold rain. The downpour had driven down leaves from the trees, and it was slippery going.

I felt damp and chilled by the time I got home. I changed into sweats and thick socks and then logged on. I had e-mails from Griffin and Gary. I opened Griffin's first.

TO: Wordpainter
FROM: Thebeast
RE: Cheating Ring
Monster news! Can't you just go to

school and go to class and eat lunch like a normal person?

Okay, first of all. You're better at kicking yourself than anybody I know. You gotta lose the I'm-pond-scum stuff. We all lust for glory in our secret hearts. It's the kids who step on bodies to get to the glory who stink. And that's never you.

Second. I know you'll trap the stinky skunks. My question is—What's the real deal? What's in their heads? Are they lazy? Afraid to fail? Under mondo pressure? Or do they just think you can buy everything?

I felt instantly better about the whole weird day. Griffin makes me feel like a normal human being. Well, almost normal. And he comes at things in a whole different direction than I do. He likes to get under someone's skin. He's a character guy. Not me. Plot and action are my thing. No touchy-feely stories for me. I attacked the keyboard.

TO: Thebeast
FROM: Wordpainter

Whoa, pass me a hanky, Mr. Sensitive. The point is to snag the cheaters. Do I care what's going on in their feeble

brains? Cheating is wrong—end of story. And btw, okay, I'll stop kicking myself. It's so hard on the feet.

After I sent Griffin the response, I opened up Gary's e-mail.

TO: Wordpainter
FROM: Allstar

Here's the 411 on Natalie Klein. When I asked if I could borrow her math notes to study for Lanigan's test, her jaw dropped about six inches. She'd totally spaced out on the test. She actually thanked me for reminding her. Not only that, she has art second period. I checked with my bud Jeremy—he's in her class. Her alibi is solid. He has a wicked crush on Nat, and stared at her the whole period.

As for the green socks, she was barefoot—I interviewed her at the pool. But I think we can cross her off our list anyway.

I headed downstairs looking forward to a Chinese calorie-loading experience.

Gram is definitely on my Top Ten Best Things In Life list, no question. But I have to admit that things don't always run like clockwork at home. When Gram is cooking on the computer, nothing is cooking in the kitchen. And housework tends to be forgotten. Totally forgotten. We're talking amnesia.

But then again, what's the point of making your bed when you're going to mess it up again that night? And who wants to chase dust bunnies around a room when you could be covering a breaking story instead?

Somehow we manage to eat our three squares and wear clean clothes most of the time. And we have this sort of conspiracy thing going, where we don't tell my ultra-organized parents how we're basically stumbling along without them.

The downside is that sometimes in the mornings, Gram and I are digging out socks from the hamper because nobody did the laundry. The upside is takeout for dinner. Chinese food, pizza, the Thai place on Main, chicken parmigiana sandwiches from Mario's—there's nothing like takeout.

Especially when your day has been a total dud.

I spilled the whole story to Gram over Kung Pao Chicken that night. I loved having her undivided attention.

"Cheating," she mused as she dished rice onto her plate. "Funny how that word came up a lot on the Hill."

She means Capitol Hill, in Washington, where she worked for years.

"I once did a piece on cheating. Profiles of cheaters." She shook her head. "How one mistake can sink your whole boat. But what's your hook?"

"No hook. I'm on the pier without a rod and reel," I said, spearing a piece of chicken with my fork. "No leads. Everyone has an alibi."

Gram sipped her tea. "But you've only done the first part of your legwork, Casey. Sure, you spoke to a few sources. But did you verify the facts? Did you check out their alibis?"

"But everything hangs together," I protested. "Kids can't just walk out of class."

Gram stole a piece of red pepper off my plate with her chopsticks and chewed it thoughtfully. "I once had a source who passed himself off as a doctor. Turned out the only medical training he had was a first-aid class for his Boy Scout merit badge."

"So maybe someone is lying?" I asked.

Gram shrugged. "I don't know. That's your job."

"Okay," I said, beginning to feel more cheerful. "Any other advice?"

"You brought it up yourself," Gram told me, pointing at me with her chopsticks. "How did the test get stolen in the first place? You can't say it's impossible because *it happened.* It's up to you to figure out how. Who got to that briefcase? How did they open it? When?"

"You're right!" I cried. I had forgotten this essential question in my focus on getting the Sock Girl. "You're so awesome, Gram."

"Like, totally," she said dryly. "And Casey? Something else. While you're figuring out the who, what and when, don't forget about the *why*." She reached over and grabbed a piece of Kung Pao chicken from my plate. "Sometimes, sweetie, you skimp on the *why*s."

"But the why is so obvious," I said, shrugging. It was bad enough that Griffin had brought up the why issue. Did I have to hear it from Gram, too? "Somebody took the easy way out for a good grade. Period."

"Not that I want to edit your copy, but you've got to watch those 'periods,' sweetie," Gram said lightly. "You can leave a lot of information out if the period comes too soon."

"There's no excuse for cheating!" I said.

"I'm not talking excuses," Gram said. "I'm talking reasons." She lifted another piece of chicken off my plate with her chopsticks and popped it into her mouth.

Note to self:

Learn how to use chopsticks. Makes it easier to steal food off someone else's plate.

Girl Reporter Walks in Weasel Boy's Shoes

I USUALLY LISTEN to every piece of advice from Gram. But this time I resisted. In my humble opinion puzzling out *whys* only slowed you down. And I had no time to waste.

Cheating was wrong. I'd never done it. Never even felt tempted. I'm not a wizard, but school has been pretty easy for me so far. It's generally the boredom—not the challenge—that gets me into trouble.

Plus, I couldn't understand how a student could feel good about an A they got by cheating. Let's face it—half of the fun of getting an A is crowing about it.

After dinner I made notes on my two-pronged attack for the next day:

Find out Mr. Lanigan's routine—when could the answer key have been stolen? Double-check alibis of Jessica, Phoebe and Angela!!!!

Then, I had an inspiration:

*****!!!!! If girl-in-green-socks didn't get the answer key yesterday, wouldn't she still want it? When and how would she get it again? Test thief doesn't know he was caught, so maybe he'll go for same place, same time?

It made sense. The person selling the test answers—Weasel Boy—probably picked the time and place because it was convenient. Under "double-check alibis," I added:

Stake out Stu Act Rm again, same time

On the other hand, Weasel Boy had to know something went wrong. If the answer key hadn't landed in the right backpack, he must figure that it had found its way into someone else's hands.

Maybe Griffin was on the right track. I needed to walk in Weasel Boy's stinky shoes for a minute. I cracked open my journal and wrote:

What are you thinking, Weasel Boy?

a. The test was ditched by some kid who didn't have a clue what it meant.

b. Some lucky kid has a free answer key.

Whatever Weasel Boy suspected, I hoped he was stupid enough to keep on peddling his stolen test.

I fingered the Tibetan river stones on my desk and then stacked them on top of the hunk of concrete from the Berlin Wall. Between Gram and my globe-trotting parents, my room was like a stop on the "It's a Small World" ride in Disney World. I have Indonesian shadow puppets and a Chinese kite and a bedspread woven in Peru. Sometimes all that color and imagination from other cultures can really kick-start my brain.

I waited for inspiration to strike. And waited. And waited. Zippo. Losing patience, I turned on my computer. I hate waiting.

I entered Gram's name in this awesome search engine that Gram let me load onto my computer. A whole list of articles popped up, and I scrolled through them. I clicked on the title "Cheaters: Dirty Deeds, Tarnished Lives."

Published in the *New York Times* Sunday magazine, the story profiled people who were caught at deceptions. A congressman who'd cheated the people he represented by channeling state money into his homes and vacations. A woman who lied about her age to enter a beauty pageant. Two students caught cheating on college exams. A basketball player who confessed that he deliberately did not score to get a payoff from gamblers.

I frowned. Gram described their actions. Their punishments. And their regrets. She showed how cheating shook up their lives. And somehow, she made me care about these people—people who had made selfish, dishonest choices—without excusing their behavior. She wrote about the different pressures they felt, and how lost and confused they had become.

In other words, the *why*s. Gram is big on finding the gray when it's so much easier to see issues in black and white. I hate that.

Black and white. Love the idea. You're right or you're wrong. In or out. On or off. Up or down.

Good or bad. It's so . . . easy. I hate gray. Gray gets messy. Who says there has to be more than one answer to a question? Keep it simple, I say. That's one reason I like journalism. So much of it is black and white.

Gram's story was still glowing on the screen when the phone rang. I snatched it up.

"Casey?" It was Megan. "I was just wondering if there was any news. I'm kind of going crazy here."

"We've got the suspects narrowed down to three," I told her. Quickly, I filled her in on everything the *Real News* crew had done.

"Wait a second," Megan said. "Phoebe and Jessica are my friends."

"And your point is . . ."

"You can't frame one of my friends just to get me off the hook," Megan warned.

"Whoa! I'm not framing anybody!" I shot back furiously. "I'm—"

"Just because you don't trust people doesn't mean—"

"Hold on," I interrupted. "Let me get this straight. Are you telling me to back off an investigation because you're friends with the kids who could be involved?"

There was a short silence. "No," Megan said hesitantly. I pictured her biting her lip the way she does when she's worried. She was probably dressed in pink flowered pajamas, with pink fluffy slippers and a matching robe. "It's just that I know Jessica can't be guilty. I-I told her what happened."

"You did? Are you nuts?" I exploded. "It will be all over the school!"

"I didn't tell her the details," Megan said defensively. "I just said I was in trouble with Ms. Nachman for something I didn't do. She was totally sympathetic."

"I'll bet," I said sourly.

"But don't you see?" Megan said eagerly. "This proves that it couldn't be her. If she were guilty, she'd figure out I was talking about Mr. Lanigan's test. Or at least she'd wonder. She wouldn't let me take the blame."

"That's *exactly* what she'd do," I cried. I didn't trust that full-of-herself mirror gazer for a second. I wondered yet again what Megan saw in her.

"You just don't get it, Casey," Megan said angrily. "She's my *friend,* okay?"

"Now you're starting to talk like her, *okay*?" I said scornfully. "Get over it, Megan. This isn't about your *feelings*. Jessica is guilty."

"Now who's going on feelings?" Megan countered. "You're letting your feelings tell you what to believe. Funny how you'll do it for Jessica, but you won't do it for me. With me, your feelings don't count. Only your *facts*."

This was gratitude? I'd spent the better part of my day trying to clear Megan and *this* is what I got? Anger raced through me. "Listen, Megan. It's time you got it through your super-duper brain that I'm trying to *help* you. Not only am I going to clear you, I'm going to have a page-one scoop for *Real News*. I thought you'd be happy."

"Well, I'm not!" Megan said. "I just want the truth."

"Are you sure you can *handle* the truth?" I snapped.

"Are you sure *you* can?" she shot back.

We both slammed down the phone.

Flinging open my journal, I wrote furiously.

Note to self: The next time you get involved in someone else's problems . . . Don't!

School Office to Be Site of World Series

AS SOON AS I calmed down, I called Toni's beeper number. She had about five million baby-sitting jobs, so she was never home. While I waited for her to call back, I sent an e-mail message to Gary, asking him to double-check Angela's alibi. Toni called as I was sending Gary's message, and I asked her to double-check Phoebe's alibi.

I checked off the list in my journal.

Angela ✓

Phoebe ✓

Jessica . . .

I wanted to check up on Princess Vanity myself. I called Ringo and asked him to meet me in the front lobby of school early the next morning.

"Oday," he said. "I'll be dere."

"Huh?"

"It's my doze," he said.

"It's your what?"

"I'll be dere!" he yelled, and hung up.

The rain stopped overnight, and a blue sky greeted me on Wednesday morning. I decided it was a good omen as I pulled on my favorite baggy green cotton sweater and jeans. I laced up my orange hightops and ran downstairs to say good-bye to Gram. I was ready for action.

"Interesting combo," Gram said. She looked over her half-glasses at my outfit, from my orange sneakers to my green sweater.

"You haven't even seen my socks." I pulled up my jeans to reveal purple socks. "Awesome."

Gram grinned. "You go, girl."

I headed out for school. What can I say about my fashion sense? Life is much more exciting when your colors clash.

I was waiting for Ringo, one orange sneaker tapping, when Mr. Baxter tramped into the office.

"Good morning, Casey," he called, moving straight to the wall of teacher mailboxes.

"Mr. Baxter! What happened to you yesterday?" I asked, trotting after him.

"Root canal," he muttered. "High-tech torture for the forty-something sophisticate."

"We need to talk," I said, glancing over at the teachers and aides milling around. "But not here."

Mr. Baxter took a sheaf of papers out of his mailbox. Then we moved into a quiet corner of the copy room off the main office. "Megan told me that you're trying to uncover this cheating thing," Mr. Baxter said in a low voice. "I'm glad to see you kids rallying together."

I nodded. "But she told me you want to call off this week's issue of the paper. Which does not work for me. We can do it, Mr. Baxter. We've got all the stories we talked about yesterday morning. And if I expose these cheaters, we'll have a huge front-page story!"

"Oh . . ." Mr. Baxter seemed disappointed. "I thought you were trying to clear Megan. Or is it the story you're pursuing?"

I frowned. Why do adults always underestimate us? "I'm going to do both. When I uncover the cheating ring, it's going to be hot. A story that can't wait a few weeks," I said firmly.

"At the moment *Real News* doesn't have an editor," he pointed out.

"We'll work extra hard. The rest of us will pitch in."

Mr. Baxter touched his square jaw gingerly

and grunted. It was a tough call. Either that, or he was still feeling tooth pain.

"Hey, I'm not here to stop the presses," he said finally, putting his mail into his satchel. "If you can get an issue together, I'm all for it. Just make it a good one."

"We will," I promised.

Easier said than done.

I spotted Ringo outside school, meandering up the footpath. Actually, I spotted the bandage before I saw Ringo. It covered his entire nose.

"Stylin' new look," I said.

He winced and touched the bandage. "It's less swollen than last night. Gary threw me a pass yesterday while we were playing basketball, and I missed. Well, my *hands* missed. My *nose* didn't."

Batter Up?

"I hope that's the end of basketball for you," I said decisively.

He nodded. "Today is baseball day." He held up a ball and bat. "I'm hoping that smaller ball equals less injury. What do you think?"

"Just watch out for the bat," I said, eyeing it. "In your hands it could become a lethal weapon. Aren't you ready to bag this lame training program yet?"

"Nah," Ringo said. "No pain, no gain."

I groaned. "*Please* don't start talking like a jock, Ringo. I'll have to kill you."

We started up the stairs. "Gary isn't so bad," Ringo said. "He's spent a lot of time trying to coach me." He pointed to his nose. "He felt really bad when I got hurt. He even bought me a soda when it was all over. Not that I could taste much. Isn't it weird, how you can't taste without your nose?"

"Ringo, when are you going to drop the jock school? When your head is knocked off?" I imagined Ringo bandaged from head to toe, with only his eyes visible. Knowing Ringo, this fate seemed pretty likely.

"I figure I need to decide by Friday." He grinned. "Cheerleading tryouts."

"Is that a threat?" I asked.

"Come on, Casey," Ringo said. "You've got to

admit that there are some killer moves in cheerleading."

"How can I, since I'm allergic to football games?" I asked. I wanted to spend more time getting Ringo to see the light, but I had more pressing concerns to deal with. "So can you spare a few minutes from your sports obsession to help out a friend?"

"That's why I'm here," Ringo said. "Spill."

"We've got to double-check Jessica's alibi," I explained as I led the way to the admin office. "I need you to create a diversion in front of Ms. Kiegel." Ms. Kiegel is manager, drill sergeant and traffic cop of the admin office. "Give me a chance to go through the late passes from yesterday."

Ringo stopped. "You want me to divert Ms. Kiegel? Whoa. Why don't you ask me to do something easy, like dive off the roof of the school into a cup of water?"

"Okay, she's tough," I said. "But I totally trust you, Ringo. When it comes to spacey behavior, you're the champ."

"I am *so* not getting comfort from that," Ringo grumbled.

Ms. Kiegel was filing when we walked into the office. She nodded grimly at us. Since we're always traipsing through the office to get supplies for *Real News*, she knows our faces and our names.

But she still makes you feel like you're trespassing on private property.

I winked at Ringo.

"Ms. Kiegel? I found this," Ringo said, holding up the bat and ball. "Can I put them in lost and found or something?"

"I don't know about the 'or something,' but you can put them in lost and found," Ms. Kiegel said.

"Cool," Ringo said. He started to wriggle out of his backpack while he held out the bat and—

How do I describe what happened next? At the risk of sounding like one of those jock commentators, let me try.

WHAM! Bat hits coffee cup.

Coffee spills.

Ms. Kiegel jumps up.

Casey edges toward the tray of late passes. . . .

"Ringo!" Ms. Kiegel cried.

"Whoa, sorry! Let me get that," Ringo said, lunging at the cup. He slipped. His arms flew out and knocked into a potted plant as tall as Ms. Kiegel. It began to totter, then fall toward her.

"Oh!" she gasped, flailing in the jungle of spidery leaves.

This was my chance. I leaped to the tray of late passes and dug in.

"Just . . . stand . . . still!" Ms. Kiegel ordered

Ringo, who had somehow managed to lodge the bat in the slats of her desk chair.

While Ms. Kiegel righted the plant, I went through the passes one by one. Bingo!

Jessica Rundel 10:15
Excuse: Doctor's Note

Second period ended at 10:50. I stuffed the passes back in the tray, and I gave Ringo the all-clear signal.

He untangled the bat and wiped up the coffee with some tissues. Then he poured some water from Ms. Kiegel's Evian bottle into the plant.

"See? All better. I'll get out of your hair now."

"That would make my day," Ms. Kiegel said, dazed. "What about the bat and ball?"

"How's this for dumb?" Ringo said. "I just remembered—they're mine!"

We made tracks out into the hall before she could respond. As soon as we were out of sight, I gripped Ringo's sleeve.

"Talk about lethal weapons! You were great," I said. "And guess what? Jessica got back to school at ten fifteen, way before second period was over. She had plenty of time to meet the guy in the Equipment Room!"

"Whoa," Ringo said. "Do you think it was her?"

"Do pigs fly?" I said.

Ringo's gray eyes were thoughtful. "If they're small enough. I was on a flight once, and there were two piglets. They rode in a little cardboard box under this guy's seat."

I grabbed his shirt. "Focus, flyboy! Jessica is guilty. I know she is. Now all I have to do is squeeze a confession out of that lemon."

At our lunchtime status meeting, Toni rushed in late. She dropped her backpack on Dalmatian Station with a crash.

"Check this out," she said. "Phoebe Trippett is in Mrs. Maroni's social-studies class, right? Well, they all went to the library to work on their projects yesterday at second period."

"Aha!" Gary waved a corn chip. "Phoebe could have slipped away without anybody seeing her."

I pushed my sandwich away. Here's a piece of advice: Leftover Kung Pao chicken and rye bread just don't mix. "That's bogus," I said. "She wouldn't be able to do that."

"Sure she would," Toni said as she unwrapped her sandwich. Turkey on pita. Was it dry-lunch day? "It's not hard. The library is always crowded, and Mrs. Maroni wasn't keeping track. I asked."

I sighed and sunk my face into my hands. I still knew Jessica was the guilty one. I knew it in my bones. But now we had *two* solid suspects.

"What about Angela?" I asked through my fingers.

"I checked her out," Gary said. "She never left science lab. I spoke to her lab partner."

"Well, at least we're down to two suspects," Toni said. She took a bite of her sandwich. "What's next?" she asked with her mouth full.

"Not to bring up unpleasant subjects," Ringo said. "But what about *Real News*? I'm ready to do layout, but can I just point something out? I, uh, don't have anything to lay out. And we're supposed to have things under control by tomorrow."

Toni swallowed. "We still haven't picked the photos for the before-and-after essay."

"And you have to check the spelling of those names in the Debate Squad caption," Ringo reminded her, waving a potato chip.

"I went over Phoebe's article," Gary said. "She's going to make a few changes and give it back to me later today. But we still don't have a page one." He looked at me. They all looked at me.

"We will," I promised. I crossed my fingers on my lap. "The cheating-ring story is just about to break. I feel it."

"You know what Megan would say," Gary said. "We need a backup story just in case yours doesn't pan out."

It was bad enough to have Megan hounding me. Now I had to have Gary, too?

"How's the Cal Pillson story coming along?" I asked him pointedly.

Gary scowled. "I'm working on it." He balled up his aluminum foil and tossed it at the trash can across the room. It rattled inside. "Two points!"

Toni and I exchanged a disgusted glance. Gary ignored us and kept moving the trash can across the room so that he could practice what I called Bogus Basketball. Then he made cheering noises when he tossed something in. I'm telling you, boys are just a completely different species from girls.

Ringo looked around the table. "We are so lost without Megan. It reminds me of when I was a kid and I lost my mom at the mall. The assistant manager gave me a hot pretzel. The kind with all that salt. Whenever I eat a pretzel, I feel kind of lost."

"Stop, Ringo," Toni said, rolling her eyes. "You're breaking my heart."

"Come on, guys," I said, remembering my promise to Mr. Baxter. "We can do this without Megan."

Ringo reached into his backpack and pulled

out a bag of pretzels. "Uh-oh. It's a message from the cosmos."

"Speaking of Megan, what about her editorial?" Gary chimed in, bringing the trash can back and sitting down. "Somebody has to write it."

Everyone looked at me. Again.

"All right," I grumbled. Actually, it was kind of nice they assumed I would write it. Not unexpected, maybe—I was a world-class reporter, after all—but nice all the same. "I'll come up with something. And I'll write that story on Congress for backup on page one."

Toni wrinkled her nose. "Wake me up when it's over."

"I thought Megan ditched that idea," Gary said.

"We cannot publish a paper without including one story that reaches beyond this school. In two months the debate squad and the basketball scores will be old details. But the U.S. Congress is a living, breathing body that—"

"Okay, okay!" Gary waved me off. "Write the piece. Just try not to make it sound like a civics lesson, okay?"

Frustrated, I squeezed the lobe of one of my perfect ears. Talk about pressure. I cracked open my journal and added the story to my list of things to do:

1. Write blow-your-socks-off editorial.
2. Study for math test.
3. Nail cheaters, clear Megan and write killer story (Bonus points for this 3-in-1 item!).
4. Write backup story on Congress. Make it sing.

All by Friday. No problem.

"Meanwhile, I've got to come up with a way to trap Weasel Boy."

"Say what?" Toni asked.

"The seller of the test. How are we going to catch the rat?"

"I don't know about you," Ringo said, peeking at the rest of his lunch. "But the only way I know to catch a rat is to put out some really stinky cheese."

"That's it!" I cried, jumping up. "Ringo, you're a genius!"

"No," Ringo said. "Just hungry."

I ran over to a PC. I logged onto the on-line student bulletin board and posted this message:

Heeeeelllp! Anybody out there have some solid notes for Lanigan's 6th grade math class? Will trade

```
anything. I've got to pass, and
I'm in mondo trouble. Hey, if I
was a whale, I'd beach myself.
```

Then I signed the message with my e-mail address, "Wordpainter."

"Hi, guys," a soft voice said.

We all turned. Megan stood in the doorway.

"How's everything going?" she asked us. She looked at me, but she looked *through* me somehow. She was still upset. With *me*.

Obviously our argument had not cleared up overnight by itself. I felt guilty, even though I knew I hadn't done anything wrong. Well, okay. Maybe I'd snapped at Megan, but she'd snapped at me, too. We were equally guilty of Snapping with Intent.

"Super!" Ringo said, using Megan's favorite word.

"We're really cooking," Toni said, pasting a smile on her face.

"Oh," Megan said. "I just wanted to make sure. I mean, I'm supposed to stay away. But if you need me . . ."

"Got it totally covered," Gary said.

I did not say anything. I figured three lies just about covered it. "Oh. Good." Megan turned and drifted off like a ghost. She was so pale that she *looked* like a ghost.

Toni shook her head. "People are talking. And Megan knows it." Toni has built-in gossip radar.

"Do kids know what happened?" I asked her.

"They don't have the facts," Toni said. "But they know she's in big trouble with Ms. Nachman. Sometimes rumors are worse than facts. They get their own spin going, and your rep gets trashed."

I thumped my hand on the desk. "Jessica!"

"What about her?" Toni asked.

I remembered how Megan had confided in Jessica. Now rumors were flying. Some friend.

I grabbed my backpack and started toward the door.

"Casey." Toni waved a few photos at me. "We're not finished here!"

"Later," I called. It was time to squeeze some answers out of Jessica Rundel.

Student Melts Under Skin Rash

I FOUND JESSICA surrounded by her friends in the cafeteria. A girl like Jessica was always with other people. She'd disintegrate if she had to spend any time alone.

The girls were talking in low voices. Probably trashing Megan.

"Hey, Jessica," I said. "Can I talk to you?"

Jessica shrugged, but didn't say anything. Obviously I didn't deserve a verbal reply.

"I'm going to get another soda," Kelli Catrice said.

"Me, too," Suki Yamura agreed. They both made a beeline toward carbonated heaven.

"I'm in real trouble in Lanigan's class," I told Jessica, sitting down. "I mean, truly lost. And I've got to ace that test. Can you help me out?"

Jessica stared at me. "Wait a second. Are you asking to borrow my math notes or something?"

"I really need help," I said.

She flipped her hair behind her shoulder. "Then I suggest you, like, study, okay? Like the rest of us. I *never* lend my notes."

What a jerk! I leaned closer. "Have you heard the rumors about Megan?"

She fiddled with the top button of her yellow cardigan. "I've heard *some* things. She's in trouble, but nobody knows why."

"Somebody who's really malicious must have started the rumors," I said, eyeballing her. "I think it's awful how people talk about other people behind their backs, don't you?"

"Maybe the person was concerned," Jessica said nervously. "You know, about Megan."

I shook my head sadly. "They were probably secretly jealous. Maybe they even wanted to hurt Megan. Because now the whole school is talking, and Megan is miserable."

"Look, it's none of your business, okay?" Jessica said, tossing her hair. "Megan has *real* friends, like Kelli and me. We've known her, like, forever. We'll support her. She doesn't need you—or those dweeby pencil-necks on the newspaper staff."

That's when it hit me. Jessica was jealous of the time Megan spent with me. Did that give her a motive? Was she letting Megan take the rap to keep her away from *Real News*? That seemed too low-down mean, even for Jessica.

"Well, guess I'd better get back to the pencil-necks," I said.

Jessica smirked.

I stood up. Then I did a double take and leaned in to study her skin. I frowned.

Jessica touched her cheek nervously. "What is it?"

"Gosh," I said. "Maybe you should make another appointment with that doctor. It looks like your rash might be spreading."

Jessica squeaked. She shot up from the chair and dashed toward the girls' room.

What can I say? You get your thrills when you can.

I'd struck out with Jessica. So far. But I still had the stakeout ahead of me. I would be late for my fifth-period class, but I didn't care.

I hurried through the halls to the Student Activities Room. I peeked in the window. It was empty. I slipped inside and closed the door softly. I looked over at the storage unit.

A backpack was there! In the exact spot Megan's had been.

My heart began to pound. I crouched down

behind a low, long bookcase that served as a room divider.

Come on, Jessica! Show your spotty face!

The door creaked open. Footsteps. Then a rustle, as though someone had picked up the backpack. I peeked over the bookcase.

It was Phoebe.

Gotcha!

I SPRANG UP. “Phoebe, hi!”

Phoebe turned, startled. A deep-red flush stained her neck and rose to her cheeks. She clutched a paper she’d taken out of the backpack.

“Hey, is that for *Real News*?” I asked, still moving toward her. “Gary told me you’d be handing it in today. Don’t look so worried. I’m sure it’s fine. I’ll take a look, if you want.”

“N-no, that’s—” Phoebe stammered, hurrying to stuff the paper back in her backpack.

“Don’t be so shy!” Without giving her a chance to say anything, I grabbed the paper out of her hands. I looked down at . . .

The answer key! Bingo!

"It's *you*!" I said. "You bought the answers to Lanigan's test!"

"I don't—"

"Don't bother," I said, cutting her off. "Maybe we should go for a little walk to Ms. Nachman's office. Ready?"

I expected Phoebe to crumble. Maybe even cry. But she surprised me. She lifted her chin and regarded me with cool green eyes.

"I don't know how that paper got into my backpack," she said.

"Do you really expect me to believe that?" I scoffed. "Not only are you a cheat, you're a liar."

But my words didn't faze her. "I don't care what you believe, Casey," she said evenly.

"You bought this test!" I cried. "I overheard you. You met someone in the Equipment Room."

Phoebe flushed. But then her eyes narrowed. "You *overheard* me? But you didn't *see* me, did you? How do you know it was me if you didn't see me?"

Rage made me boil over. I knew I shouldn't tell anyone Megan's secret. But I couldn't help it. I needed all the ammunition I could get. "You know those rumors around school about Megan?" I said. "They're all true. Megan is in trouble because Ms. Nachman thinks she bought the test. It was in her backpack, and Mr. Lanigan saw it. Somebody left the test in there, thinking it was *your* backpack."

"Wait a second, Casey," Phoebe said slowly. "Let me get this straight. I just told you that that's exactly what happened to me. How come you believe Megan and you don't believe me? Because Megan is your friend?"

"Because you have green socks!" I yelled.

"You're crazy." Phoebe grabbed the paper out of my hand and tore it into little pieces. "And now it's your word against mine."

"I thought Megan was your friend," I said furiously. "How can you let her take the blame?"

For the first time Phoebe looked unsure of herself. "I'm sorry for Megan. But she won't get in trouble. Everyone knows she wouldn't cheat."

"Ms. Nachman doesn't," I said. "And I'm going to tell her that you're the cheat."

Phoebe shrugged. "Go ahead."

"I'm warning you, Phoebe," I said, taking a step toward her. "I'm putting the pressure on, starting now."

The fifth-period bell rang. A strange half smile flitted over Phoebe's face.

"Pressure doesn't scare me, Casey," she said softly. "It's my life."

She turned and walked out of the room. I just

stared at the empty air for a minute. I'd caught her red-handed. How had Phoebe turned that whole situation around?

I left the room in a daze . . . and bumped smack into Ms. Nachman.

"Whoa, Casey." She put her hands on my shoulders to steady me. "What are you doing in the hall between classes? Do you have a pass?"

"I'm investigating," I said breathlessly.

Ms. Nachman frowned at me. "I made it clear that any 'investigating' would *not* interfere with classes. Correct?"

"Yes," I said impatiently. "But I have a suspect. I'm really close to breaking the story, Ms. Nachman."

"Do you know who bought the test?" Ms. Nachman asked. "Do you have proof? Did some-one confess?"

I squirmed. "Not yet," I said. "But I'm getting closer. Just now I—"

I was about to tell Ms. Nachman about Phoebe, but she held up a hand to stop me. "I need proof, Casey," she said carefully. "That's why I'm giving Megan O'Connor the benefit of the doubt at the moment. And I don't want another student's name to be blackened because of cir-cumstantial evidence. It will make a bad situation worse. At this point we just have to hang tight and hope that Megan—or whoever bought the test—tells us they did it and points the finger at who stole it. So if and when you come to me, I want you to bring either hard evidence or a confession. Okay?"

"Okay," I said, downcast. I wanted to blurt out everything I knew about Phoebe. But I couldn't prove she'd bought the test any more than Megan could prove she hadn't. Somehow I didn't think lime-green socks would clinch the story for Ms. Nachman.

Mrs. Nachman checked her watch. "Now I'll walk you to class and smooth things over with your teacher. But this is the first, last and only time I'll do that. Got it?"

Glumly I trudged down the hall beside Ms. Nachman. Things seemed to have gotten worse instead of better. I'd been hot on the trail of the wrong suspect. . . . Sorry, Jessica! Remind me to apologize sometime . . . like, never.

And the *right* suspect had wiggled out from underneath my grasp like a slimy lizard.

I had to find a way to get Phoebe to confess, or I had to discover the identity of the thief. And I had to do it soon. Time was running out.

Thief Has Feet of Clay

THE REST OF THE day dragged like the last hour before Christmas vacation. On my way out I stopped at the *Real News* office to check my e-mail on the computer. Zilch. No answer to my posting. But Ringo had left me a note, saying to stop by the sports field to fill him in on any news. So I did.

I watched while Gary threw a pass to Ringo, who ran backward to get underneath

So? Is half-time one-fourth of double-time?

it. He positioned himself carefully . . .

Then dropped the ball on his toe.

"It's time to stop the madness, Gary," I called as I walked over. "Can't you just let Ringo be Ringo?"

Ringo trotted toward us from the outfield. "I think I'm getting the hang of it," he said. "I just have one suggestion. They should make the ball bigger." He looked at his mitt. "Or maybe the glove should be bigger. What do you think?"

Gary only sighed.

"I'm with you, Ringo," I said. "If we were meant to catch balls, we'd have glue on our hands."

"Is there some reason you're here?" Gary asked me. "Or is it just to bug me?"

"Whoa, look!" Ringo suddenly cried. His gaze was stuck on the cheerleaders, who were at the other end of the field. "Look at that move! A classic double-full twist rotation."

I glanced over. All I saw were bouncing girls. They made some sort of pyramid, and a girl did a pretty nifty back somersault off the pile.

"How did you—" I started. But suddenly, Ringo did a series of three back handsprings that ended in a perfect split.

Gary and I gaped at him. "How did you learn to do that?" I asked.

Ringo sprang to his feet and dusted off his hands. "Megan's friend Kelli has been giving me lessons," he said.

"Not Kelli!" I cried. "Ringo, you're doomed to the Barf Zone."

Gary turned to me. "Maybe it *is* hopeless. Our guy has a major aptitude for all things girly. I mean, first he takes pottery lessons, and now this."

"Girly?" I said. "Watch it, buddy. That word makes my skin crawl. Anyway, plenty of guys are cheerleaders. Just not at Trumbull. Not so far."

"Actually, I'm pretty bad at pottery," Ringo said. "My teapot collapsed the other day. Now it's just a blob. Not that there's anything wrong with blobs. Blobs can be cool."

"I didn't know you were into ceramics," I said to him.

Gary rolled his eyes. "He joined the Craft Club. Can you believe it? He's a lost cause."

"Mr. Lanigan told me not to be discouraged," Ringo said cheerfully. "He was absolute coolness, actually. Not to mention that he looks pretty stylin' in an apron."

Something *ping*ed in my brain. "Mr. Lanigan is in charge of Craft Club?" I asked slowly. "And he wears an apron? Over his jacket?"

"Not Mr. Lanigan!" Gary put his hands over his ears. "In ruffles and bows? I can't take it."

"It doesn't have ruffles or anything," Ringo explained. "It's like a butcher's apron."

"Does he take off his jacket?" I asked again.

Ringo nodded. "Sure. You can get pretty gunky working with clay. We all hang up our sweaters and stuff in that big closet in the back of the art room."

"Why didn't you tell me this before?" I exclaimed.

"Because the teapot was going to be your Christmas present," Ringo said. "Um, by the way, how do you feel about blobs?"

"What's up, Casey?" Gary asked. "Your nose is turning pink."

"Don't you guys get it?" I asked excitedly. "Mr. Lanigan takes off his jacket! He hangs it in a closet."

Gary and Ringo exchanged puzzled glances. "And that means . . . what?" Gary asked.

"He's neat?" Ringo supplied.

I started off the field. I didn't have time to explain.

"Where are you going?" Ringo called.

"To check the Craft Club names," I shouted. "Come on!"

I thundered up the stairs to the *Real News* office. Gary and Ringo were hot on my heels. I booted up the PC.

"Power surge," Ringo said, flopping down at Dalmation Station. "I think I've clicked onto it. You're thinking that Mr. Lanigan's jacket in the closet means someone could get his keys, open his briefcase and get the test."

"Exactly."

"But wouldn't Mr. Lanigan notice if someone disappeared into the closet?" Gary asked as we waited for the PC files to pop up.

"Probably not," Ringo said. "Everybody's working on their own stuff, and looking at everybody else's stuff, and going up front to get more clay. It's total chaos. Mr. Lanigan gets into it. Even button-down dudes need a creative outlet. I don't think he'd notice."

"The person would have to get the test, Xerox it, and then slip it back in his briefcase," I said, clicking on Megan's club files. "That's the hard part."

"But the art room is right next to the Xerox machine," Ringo pointed out. "It would only take a minute."

"*If* the thief knew the test was in the briefcase, and the keys were in the pocket," Gary said.

"Which they could," I pointed out. "Everyone

knows Mr. Lanigan monitors the Math Resource Room all the time. He's always talking about it in class. What if Mr. Lanigan was working on the test, and the thief walked by to look up something in the reference books behind the desk, or to throw something in the waste can? He could have seen the test on the computer screen, then watched what Mr. Lanigan did with it. The scenario could definitely work. The guy who stole it didn't do it on a whim. He's running a business. He's organized."

I leaned closer to the screen as I scrolled down the list of Craft Club members. Ringo was there. Along with a few other familiar names.

"I know Troy Chandler has Lanigan for math," I said. "He's in my class. Josh Greenbaum, too."

"Let's check the names against the class rosters," Gary suggested.

It didn't take us long to find out the overlapping names.

```
Leslie Spivey
Josh Greenbaum
Troy Chandler
Ashley Kosinski
```

"Okay, we can eliminate the two girls," I said. "We're looking for the seller of the test, and we know he's a guy."

"Wait a second," Gary said. "The person who

stole the test doesn't necessarily have to be the person who *sold* the test. That person could have passed it off to the seller."

"I didn't think of that," I said, discouraged. And, truth be told, a little annoyed I hadn't realized this first.

"And if you think about it, the person who stole the test doesn't really have to be in Lanigan's class at all," Ringo said. "They just could have seen him working on it in the Resource Center, and saw a way to make some bucks."

I eyed him. "Do you have to pick right now to get logical?"

From four suspects we'd gone to basically the whole student body. My head was spinning. There were way too many possibilities.

"You both could be right," I said finally. "But this is the place to start. The person who stole the test has to be linked to Lanigan somehow. But how can we narrow it down?"

None of us had an answer.

I headed toward my locker to get my jacket. It was time to give up and go home. Lanigan's test was in two days, and I hadn't cracked a book. Not to mention that I had a front-page story and an editorial to write. I was maxed out, and I was bummed, to boot.

As I walked down the hall, I saw Megan at her locker. My steps slowed. I hadn't really had a chance to apologize. Even though I'd been right that one of Megan's friends was involved, I probably shouldn't have bitten her head off on the phone. Besides, I'd trashed Jessica, and she turned out to be totally innocent. Well, she was still a pea-brained airhead whose mouth ran on overtime. But maybe she couldn't help herself. At least she wasn't a cheater.

I approached Megan slowly. "Hey," I said.

"Hey," she said. She took out a book and stared at it. Then she put it back in her locker. That looked like a hopeful sign to me, like she was stalling, waiting for me to talk.

"I think you should know that Phoebe is the one who bought the test," I said. "I was going to call you tonight." Quickly, I told her the story. "I'm sorry. I mean, I'm glad we've got someone on the hook. But I'm sorry that it's your friend."

"I'm sorry, too," Megan said. She leaned her forehead against her locker for a minute.

"I just don't get it," I said. "She was cornered, and she didn't even break a sweat. The girl is an ice sculpture. I can't believe she'd let you take the rap."

"Well, it's not like she's my best friend," Megan said. "I mostly know her because we both went to Millridge last year. She's not like Jessica."

I snorted. Some best friend. Thanks to big mouth Jessica, rumors were flying about Megan all over school. But I didn't want to add to Megan's problems by telling her that her best friend was a rat. And if you think I was jealous of Jessica, you're way off base. If Megan wanted to hang around with shiny-haired phonies instead of intrepid girl reporters, that was her problem.

Megan frowned thoughtfully. "Come to think of it, Phoebe's really a loner. I mean, she's in a few clubs. But it's not like we ever just hang out, or go to the mall together. I don't think she's that close with anyone."

"What is she like?" I asked curiously.

"She's really smart," Megan said. "That's why I can't believe she'd need to cheat. Her parents just separated over the summer. They split custody so she has one week with one parent, one week with another. That doesn't seem so bad, but they have her on this really strict schedule. She never gets to kick back and just hang, you know? She's always running off to lessons and tutorials."

I thought back to how Phoebe's mother had tapped her watch and snapped, "Ballet!" as though Phoebe was a trained seal. "I think I know what you mean. But that doesn't excuse what she did."

"I'm not saying that," Megan said impatiently.

"I'm just trying to figure out why she did it."

There it was again—that troublesome *why*. It just kept popping up.

"Maybe you could try talking to her," I suggested.

Megan sighed. "She totally avoided me all day today. Now I know why. Let's face it, Casey. She knows the situation. If Phoebe was going to confess, she would have done it by now."

"Look, I know I'll come up with something," I said. "I'm closing in on the seller, too."

Megan looked at me with haunted eyes.

"If we don't find out who sold the test by Friday when the Honor Council meets . . ." Her voice trailed off. "They're going to suspend me. Maybe even expel me."

"It's not going to happen, Megan," I promised. But I wished I could be sure.

"Thanks, Casey," Megan said. "Look, I'm sorry I said those things on the phone. I was just scared and freaked out."

"I'm sorry, too," I said.

One thing about apologies. They stick in your mouth. But once they're out, they feel pretty good.

"And I'm sorry about not trusting you," I added. That one was *really* hard to say. Maybe because it was so true.

"It's okay," Megan said. "I've thought about

it, and I think I get it. That's you. That's Casey. You have to question things. That's why you're a good reporter."

"And you have faith in people," I said. "That's what makes you a good person."

I faced Megan and looked her in the eye. We'd skated pretty close to the edges of friendship, I guess. I'd had plenty of wicked thoughts about Megan. And I was sure I wasn't at the top of her warm and fuzzy list. But we'd made it back to the place where we could still be ourselves and connect.

It felt good.

"I'm going to clear you, Megan," I said to her. "I promise."

I swallowed back a lump of emotion in my throat. Could I do it? I *had* to do it.

"I know you'll try your heart out, Casey," Megan said. She hoisted her backpack on her shoulder. "That's what makes *you* a good friend."

Reporter Caught with Hand in Cookie Jar

I LOOKED AT my list one more time:

THINGS TO DO—BEFORE FRIDAY

1. Write blow-your-socks-off editorial.
2. Study for math test.
3. Nail cheaters, clear Megan and write killer story (Bonus points for this 3-in-1 item!).
4. Write backup story on Congress. Make it sing.

Same list. No progress.

That night I sat down at the computer to

check my e-mail. Still no nibble from the Weasel Boy. I worked on the Congress story for a while and then tried to study. And over and over, I tried to think of a way to thaw Phoebe the Ice Queen.

I added one more item to my To Do list:

5. Send a long, witty e-mail to my best friend.

I e-mailed the whole thing to Griffin and sighed. I knew he would understand what I meant. That I was stuck. Under pressure. Overloaded.

Then I scrolled through a list of files on the computer and clicked on Gram's story about cheaters.

Something about the profile of the college student had stuck in my head.

"It didn't seem wrong at the time," Trevor recalls. "I was an A student. I'd worked hard for my grades. I belonged in the engineering program. I knew the professor wouldn't accept that I'd missed a week of studying to pledge a fraternity. Cheating was my only out. It was the only way to protect everything I'd worked so hard for."

If I combined that with the profile of the Congressman who'd cheated . . . it would make a killer editorial for this issue of *Real News*. It would tie in with the Congress story *or* the cheating-ring story.

My hands framed the keyboard. Instant editorial. Perfect editorial.

And all I had to do was block, copy, do a little rewriting and tie in old Trumbull Middle School, and put my name on it.

But it wouldn't be mine.

"Aaarrrgh!" I groaned, shaking my head madly. I couldn't lift stuff from Gram's work. How could I even consider it? I started another e-mail to Griffin.

Okay, true confession.

Gram wrote a story that would have been perfect for *Real News*. And with Megan out of the picture, I'm so overloaded that I just thought about lifting Gram's piece.

I am the lowest of lowlifes. Once upon a time I was the high and mighty judge of cheaters. But tonight, for a moment, I

actually thought about cheating. Sure, I'd never cheat on an exam.

But now, jammed up for time and crammed up in my room, it would have been so sweet to push a button and have an instant editorial.

I know. I promised I wouldn't kick myself anymore. But you can feel free. As of this moment I am bending over.

Still feeling as dirty as the gum scraped from the bottom of my sneaker, I sent the e-mail and wondered why Griffin didn't answer. Then I remembered—Wednesday night was the night Griffin went to the movies with his dad. Great. I'd be alone in my misery till tomorrow.

Unless Griffin was at home. And he'd got the e-mail. And was too repulsed to ever talk to me again. . . .

Rolling the Tibetan stones between my hands, I decided to attack the Congress article. At least, I'd be able to cross it off my list—honestly.

On Thursday morning I got a short e-mail from Griffin.

Just blow me out of the water. Since when were you ever at a loss for words?

You'll come up with the right stuff for the article. Never fear.

And straighten up, beanhead—I don't wanna kick you. You're just proving my original point. Temptation is a killer. For everybody. Now you understand the *why*. Why Phoebe did it. Why anyone might crumble under pressure. Isn't that part of being a good reporter? Walking in someone else's shoes? More later. . . .

Somehow, Griffin's message didn't make me feel much better. Okay, he didn't think I was a total loser—just human. But I don't like making mistakes. I didn't want to be human. I wanted to be right!

At school I hurried to the *Real News* office. Gary was hammering away at a PC, and Ringo was hunched over his Simon cartoons.

I handed my story on Congress to Ringo.

"Not exactly hot front-page stuff, but I hope we won't have to run it," I told him.

"I'll hold the front page until six tonight," Ringo promised. "If we want to hand out the paper on Monday, I've got to get it to the printer by lunchtime tomorrow. As it is, I'll have to come in early in the morning." Ringo rubbed both hands through his hair. "What about the editorial?" He sounded so together, it was freaky. Like someone else had invaded his body—someone from *this* planet.

"I'll get it to you by the end of the day," I promised. As soon as I figure out what to write. I hated to admit it, but Megan was a hard act to follow.

Not to mention that my last try at writing the piece had brought me dangerously close to the dark side. I still felt ashamed. Too ashamed to even mention it to Gram that morning at breakfast.

Toni walked in and dropped into a seat with a sigh. She pushed up the sleeves of her purple sweater. "It's our last day to clear Megan. Anybody got a plan?"

"Not yet," I admitted. "I keep checking my e-mail, but so far, my stinky cheese trap hasn't worked. But Megan told me more about Phoebe yesterday."

Quickly, I filled the gang in on what Megan had told me.

"I almost feel sorry for her," Toni said. She drummed her fingers on the table. Today she was wearing silver rings on almost every finger. Even her thumbs. "Don't get me wrong—I'm not cutting the girl any slack if she cheated. But her parents sound like a horror show. Everybody needs some down time."

Gary twirled around in his chair. "Pressure," he said. "Cal Pillson talks about it, too. Here's a guy who loves sports. But his father is on him all the time about going the distance, doing better, improving his stats. You can tell the guy is slammed." His caramel eyes looked thoughtful.

"Slammed," Ringo repeated. "Sports will do that to you. Slammed. And smashed. And bruised. And bonked. And—"

"Maybe we've got something here," Toni said.

"Incredibly painful sports bloopers?" Ringo asked.

"Pressure," Toni hissed. "Only we need Megan to put it together."

I was silent, for once. Everyone else had zeroed in on the *why*s of Phoebe's behavior. They looked past the bad stuff and got to the heart of it. To what made it not just a good story, but a *great* story. Gram had told me to do that. So had Griffin. And Megan. Why hadn't I?

Because until last night, I couldn't imagine why someone would cheat.

Maybe the *why* was the key. Not toward excusing Phoebe, but understanding her. Maybe I'd pushed Phoebe too hard. Maybe I shouldn't have come on like gangbusters. The girl was used to pressure; more of it wouldn't make her cave.

But maybe sympathy would bring her around. She could confess. Megan would be cleared. I'd have my story.

And a clear conscience. If Phoebe lived in a pressure cooker, at least I wouldn't have to put on the lid.

"So Toni, did you proofread that caption?" Ringo asked. "I've got page three all set except for your photo. We have to make sure the names are all spelled right, or kids freak."

"I didn't get to it." Toni's mouth set stubbornly. Sometimes she went to this weird place and none of us could reach her. Usually I just got annoyed. Now I wondered why. I realized that Toni wanted to be let off the hook.

"Gary, let's you and me do it," I offered. "You read off the names from Megan's list, and I'll check them against the caption."

"Sure," Gary agreed. He accessed Megan's file.

Toni pushed the paper toward me. Our eyes met for a minute. She looked . . . *grateful.* I smiled at her, to let her know that whatever was bothering her, I wouldn't ask.

Whoa. The warming of my relations with Toni Velez usually proceeded with baby steps. I think we just took a normal-sized one.

"Amy Assarian," Gary called out. "A-m-y. A-s-s-a-r-i-a-n."

I checked the spelling against Megan's list. "Got it. Next."

"Troy Chandler," Gary said. "T-r—"

My head jerked up. "Hold it. Troy Chandler is on the Debate Squad?"

Toni frowned. "Not any more. Megan must have made that list up a while ago. Troy dropped out the second day."

"Do you know what this means?" I said. "Troy is on our list of possible suspects. He had a chance to steal the test and return it—he's in the Craft Club. And if Troy was on the Debate Squad, that means that Phoebe knows him. It's a connection!"

"Big whoop," Gary said. "I know Troy. He's in my English class. That doesn't mean I'd buy a test from him."

I hesitated, thinking. "And he asked Andy Chong and me on Tuesday if we were afraid we'd flunk the test. Maybe he was fishing."

"You're the one who's fishing now," Gary said.

Gary was right. I didn't have much. But I had something. I had to tackle Phoebe again.

Meanwhile, it was time for math.

"Cheater" Tattooed Across Student's Forehead

THE THURSDAY MATH review. As Mr. Lanigan wrote numbers on the board, I had to admit I wasn't feeling my most whiz-bang confident about Friday's test. And Friday was tomorrow.

But if I had the answers . . .

I looked over at Troy Chandler. He was copying down what Mr. Lanigan was writing, this totally studious expression on his face.

I studied Josh Greenbaum. He looked as lost as I did. If he had the answers, why would he look lost?

Who are you, Weasel Boy? Neither boy looked like a cheater. But then again, Phoebe didn't, either.

So I had to ask myself: What does a cheater

look like? Red-faced? Goofy grin? Beady eyes?

Get real. Like anyone. Like me.

Mr. Lanigan dusted off his hands. "Now, are there any questions before the test tomorrow?"

"Can you cancel it?" Josh asked. Everyone laughed.

Andy Chong asked a question, and the Terminator turned back to the board. I tuned out Mr. Lanigan's explanation. After all, I hadn't even understood Andy's *question.* Obviously Andy had studied his brains out, just like he'd said.

When the bell rang, I edged up to Troy. "That was funny, what Josh said before," I said.

"Yeah," he said, shoving his math book into his backpack. "Too bad Terminator didn't go for it."

"My grade is sinking faster than Titanic," I said. "Got any ideas?"

Troy's head was bent over his backpack. I waited, holding my breath.

"Yeah," he said, rising and slinging his backpack over one shoulder. "Pray."

At lunchtime I combed the cafeteria for Phoebe. No sign of her. The coward must be eating her sandwich in the girls' washroom. After an awkward peek at feet under the stalls of one girls' room, I finally caught up with Phoebe at her locker.

"What now?" she asked coldly.

I hadn't really prepared what to say. I always counted on myself to wing it. But all of a sudden I got distracted by Phoebe's locker.

Think about a locker for a minute. It's not like you spend a lot of time hanging out at it. But it's more than a place to stow your jacket and grab a textbook. It's a little corner of the school that's totally yours. It saves you from thinking you're just another cog in a twirling wheel. Just another fry in the extra-large order.

Some kids put up pictures of their friends. Some kids hang beads, or lucky charms, or posters of Leo DiCaprio. Some plaster funny bumper stickers on the inside door. Some seriously lame kids, like Gary, hang pennants of their favorite teams.

But Phoebe's locker held . . . nothing. Nothing personal, that is. Her jacket hung from a hook. Her books were stacked neatly. Taped to the door of her locker was a calendar.

I blinked. Not even an interesting calendar, with photographs of her favorite crush or of kittens or cartoons. It was just a grid—boxes full of things to do. Her after-school activities crammed almost every day, even Saturdays. French Club. French Tutorial. Oboe Lesson. Ballet. Science Club.

Leadership Workshop, whatever that was.

And one week was highlighted in pink and read "Dad's Week." One week was highlighted in yellow and read "Mom's Week."

Talk about overload!

"Earth to Casey," Phoebe said impatiently. "I'm in a hurry, okay?"

For the first time, instead of *hearing* about how overloaded Phoebe was, I could *see* it.

"I was just looking at your schedule," I said. "Do you ever have time to breathe?"

Phoebe looked away. "Just say what you came to say, Casey."

She thought I was being sarcastic. Start over.

"Look," I said. "I just want you to know that I'm pretty sure the seller is Troy Chandler."

She shrugged. "Don't know him."

"Okay, now I'm sure it's him," I said. "You just confirmed it. Because you're covering up. You *do* know Troy, and the question is, why would you lie unless I was right? He was on the Debate Squad with you for two days. That's fact number one."

Phoebe's face went blank, as if she was zoning me out.

I held up two fingers. "Here's fact number two. You're right—I didn't see you in the Equipment

Room. I saw a girl with lime-green socks. I know that you have a pair." I held up three fingers. "Fact number three, I caught you picking up your backpack at the exact time, and in the exact place, that the seller told you to. Three strikes you're out, Phoebe."

She struggled to keep her stone face. But I could tell I was getting to her this time. She looked as though she were about to cry.

"Look, I know you're under pressure," I said, nodding at the schedule. "Maybe you feel squeezed. Maybe even desperate. But that doesn't excuse what you did. And it *especially* doesn't excuse letting Megan take the fall. Your *friend*, Phoebe."

She swallowed. "So what's your point?"

"I'm not going to threaten you again," I said. "I'm just telling you that I'm going with what I have so far. I'm telling Ms. Nachman everything by the end of today. But I'm also giving you a chance to confess. I think it will be easier for you if you do."

"You can't clear Megan without my help," Phoebe said, her voice shaking. "Even if they believe you, people will always wonder if she bought that test too. And you still don't have proof against Troy."

"I have enough to make things hard for you,"

I said quietly. "But that's not the point. Don't you see? You already made one bad choice. Don't keep making it worse."

Phoebe's lower lip trembled. "It's not that easy," she whispered.

I put down my knapsack. I studied my fingernails for a second. I figured I had one chance to say what I wanted, to get Phoebe to confess, to clear Megan and maybe, just maybe, to help Phoebe. So I wanted to say it perfectly. Finally, I said, "You know, my grandmother says that we decide what kind of person we are over and over again. I never understood what she meant before, but I'm starting to now. I think it's about decisions we make every day. Little ones, big ones. They start to add up and make a person. And the person you make should match the person you want to be."

Phoebe looked down. Her hair swung against her cheek, so I couldn't see her face. I waited, hoping she would cave. At least she hadn't walked away. I could wrap everything up, snag Troy Chandler and save Megan by the end of the day.

"Phoebe, I know what it's like," I admitted. "When it looks like there's an easy way out. Like it's the only way out."

Suddenly, Phoebe turned around so fast her hair slapped my cheek. She slammed her locker door shut and took a few steps down the hall.

"I've been there, too," I called after her.

When she turned back to me, her face was as closed as ever.

"Just leave me alone, Casey," she said. Then she hurried away.

Reporter Spills Guts

I WAS MAD at Phoebe. I gave her the chance to do the right thing, and she blew it.

But now I knew something about temptation. About the need to be the smart one, the perfect one. I was ticked off at myself, too.

A fine mist of slime clouded my brain from last night's near cheat-fest. And there was only one way to chase away the haze.

I went to the pay phones in the school lobby and called home.

"Casey, aren't you supposed to be at school?" Gram asked. In the background the *plunk* of her fingers on the keyboard stopped.

"I am at school. It's lunchtime."

"Noon already?" Gram sighed. "Where did the morning go?"

"Gram, there's something I've got to tell you. . . ." My chest felt tight as I spilled my guts. That I'd been stuck for ideas. That I'd thought about stealing her work and running it under my name.

"No wonder you were moping around this morning," Gram said.

"I'm sorry."

"Well." There was a pause. I could swear I could hear Gram's brain ticking. I shifted my feet nervously, waiting for the blast. Gram never sugar-coated her opinions.

"First off, I'm flattered that you dig my work," she said crisply. "And second, you're being a bit hard on yourself. You were tempted, but you didn't cheat. No crime was committed."

I cradled the phone against my shoulder and leaned against the wall. "Then why do I feel so awful?"

"You're under pressure, sweetie," Gram said, her voice warming. "That happens to everyone. But pressure doesn't form somebody's character. It reveals it."

Another Gram-ism.

"I'm not sure I understand that," I admitted. "But I do feel better."

"Good," Gram said. "Next item—your deadlines. Let me suggest this. . . ."

◆◆◆

The newspaper office was quiet when I parked myself at a desk after school. Ringo was there, scanning Toni's photos into the computer.

"Where is everyone?" I asked.

"Gary's covering a basketball game. Toni has a baby-sitting gig. You're stuck with me." When he lifted his head, I saw a big purple bruise around his left eye.

"Another ball encounter?" I asked. He nodded. "Ringo, you're like a walking episode of *E.R.* When are you going to tell Gary to get lost?"

Ringo sighed. "It doesn't hurt. And you and Gary need to lighten up on me."

"What do you mean?" I asked, surprised. Out of everyone on the staff, Ringo seemed to take my take-no-prisoners attitude in stride.

Just then Mr. Baxter knocked on the door and popped his head in. "Are we going to have a newspaper this week?" he asked.

"Absolutely!" I said, as Ringo gave him a thumbs-up.

"We'll probably be here awhile, tucking everything in," Ringo said.

Mr. Baxter nodded. "What's our front-page story?"

Quickly, I filled him in on what I'd discovered about Phoebe. "So I'm using the school cheating scandal to illustrate the bigger issue—how everyone is tempted, at some time, to take the easy out. I'm using some research that I did—I've pulled up some great quotes from a published article. With permission from the writer, of course. There's a profile of a congressman who cheated. And an engineering student at a college. Great stuff."

I grinned. Gram had come through for me, big-time. She'd explained how I could use part of her story, as long as I gave her credit, and I'd managed to hammer out a quick draft of my story—complete with cited quotes—before the final lunch bell.

"Really?" Mr. Baxter lifted one beefy hand to his chin. "Sounds intriguing. But go with the backup story."

"What?" I sprang out of my chair.

"You can't run that cheating story," Mr. Baxter said quietly. "It's libel. Remember how I explained what that is to the staff? Any false or misleading statement that exposes a person to public ridicule or injures his or her reputation—"

"But we know the test was stolen," I protested. "And I know Phoebe is involved. I found the paper in her backpack!"

"Yeah," Ringo said. "And you found it in

Megan's. If you write about Phoebe, you have to write about Megan, too."

"Look, you did a good job, Casey," Mr. Baxter said. "You're on the right track. But we can't print it."

Ringo nodded. "That's what Megan would say."

"It's your word against Phoebe's, Casey," Mr. Baxter went on. "Journalism has to be factual. You need more than one source to verify something. Or you need witnesses. Or evidence. Or, in this story, a confession would help. But you can't print something if you don't have proof."

Boooing! It hit me between the eyes. I knew they were right.

"Okay," I said wearily. "I'll polish the Congress piece. And I'll catch Ms. Nachman before she leaves for the day."

"I'll be in the faculty lounge if you need me," Mr. Baxter said. "Probably till six or so. Think you can finish up by then?"

"Sure," Ringo said as Mr. Baxter disappeared. A moment later he added, "We may have a blank newspaper, but we'll be finished by six."

"Is it that bad?" I asked.

He shrugged. "Megan's got such a good eye for layout. I'm just afraid this is going to end up looking like a kindergarten collage."

Ringo accessed the desktop publishing program. I called up my Congress article. We both worked away for a while. Then Ringo yawned and stretched.

"Mind if I turn on the TV for a minute? I want to catch something."

I shrugged. "Sure."

Ringo leaned over and switched on Gary's little portable TV to ESPN.

I groaned. "My worst nightmare. You've turned into a Gary clone after all."

"I just wanted to see the national cheerleading competition," Ringo said.

I heard the announcer calling out strange terms like "basket toss" and "arabesques." I tried to tune it out and concentrate, but finally, I gave up. I turned and looked at the screen.

"Dig those moves," Ringo said enthusiastically. "Okay, maybe that high-stepping is on the stupid side. But you've got to admit those kids are good at it."

"They're in the Barf Zone," I grumbled. But secretly I was impressed. Maybe it *did* take athletic ability to cheerlead. Even though it was totally useless, it looked *hard.*

Then the competition was over. Ringo switched off the TV. The hum of the computers seemed oppressive. "Listen, I need some fuel," Ringo said.

"Want to grab some vending action?"

"Can't," I said. "I really have to finish this. Then I've got to catch Ms. Nachman. *Then* I've got to study for Lanigan's test. Besides, it's pizza night at the Smith house. I don't want to overload."

"Overload on junk food?" Ringo asked incredulously. "What a concept!"

Ringo left to hit the machines in the cafeteria, and I switched into the e-mail program. I was beginning to think that it was useless. Weasel Boy wasn't going to answer my posting. But it was my only lead at the moment.

I sat up with a jolt when I saw what popped up on screen:

TO: Wordpainter
FROM: easy.A
RE: gotta have it

Sounds like you really need to ace that test, Wordpainter. All you need is the cash, and a perfect score can be yours. If you're interested, meet me at school. Room 101, 4 p.m.

"Busted, Troy Chandler!" I crowed.

The Rat Takes the Cheese

ROOM 101 WAS DARK. The hallway outside was deserted. No clubs met in this part of school. I switched on the light. It was 3:55. I picked a desk in the front row to wait.

The hands of the clock crept forward. When they hit 4:15, I wondered if easy.A would show. I stood up and restlessly roamed the room. I wandered over to scan the items on the bulletin board. That's when I saw the note pinned at eye level.

> Hey, wordpainter. If you're reading this, you must be interested. Meet me downstairs in Room C-4.

Room C-4? I'd never heard of it. I headed for the stairs that went to the lower level.

I passed the gym, the athletic locker rooms

and the pool. Everything was so eerily empty. No teams were practicing today. The silence pressed against my ears. I almost missed the moronic jocks shouting, "Way to go, man!"

I followed the corridor farther than I'd ever gone. The corridor made a sharp left. There were two short steps down, and another long corridor. It wasn't very well lit.

This was janitor territory, I guessed, noting that most of the doors looked as though they led to storage. One was marked BOILER.

Room C-4 was at the very end of the corridor. My heart pounded as I pushed open the door cautiously.

"Hello?" No answer. The room was dim. The only light was from the hallway behind me. It was enough to let me see that this was a storage room. Old folding chairs were stacked in a corner, and a mop that had lost most of its strands. There was a grimy work sink beside the door.

I looked for the light switch, but I couldn't find it. I put my hand against the wall, and it came back streaked with dust. I didn't think anybody had been here in ages.

I moved forward into the room. "Anybody here? Hello?"

Suddenly I heard a noise behind me. I turned just in time to see the door slam shut.

I was immediately plunged into darkness. "Hey!" I rushed toward the door and pounded on it. "Hey! Let me out!"

"Maybe a night in there will convince you to keep your newshound nose out of my business," a male voice hissed.

It had to be Troy. I pounded against the door. "I don't know what you're talking about."

"You tried to trap me," the voice said in a low, harsh tone. "Who do you think you're fooling, Wordpainter? I know you tried to get Phoebe to confess so you could write your big story. It didn't take a genius to figure out who you were from your e-mail address."

"Listen to me, easy.A," I said. "I know what you did and I know who you are, *Troy Chandler*!"

There was a pause. Then the voice sank even lower.

"How do you know who I am? You never saw me. And you can't find anybody who admits they bought the test, can you?"

"I'm going to tell Ms. Nachman!" I yelled.

"Go ahead. Tell her. You'll just look like you're trying to protect your friend. You still don't have any proof, newsgirl!"

I slumped against the door. With my ear pressed against it, I heard his mocking laughter grow fainter and fainter as he walked away.

Girl Reporter Spends 12 Years in Broom Closet

SOME REPORTER I WAS. I couldn't even manage to put together a story, even though I knew who the bad guys were.

I pounded on the door with all my strength. But Troy wasn't coming back, and I knew it. I tried not to be scared. Ringo would notice that I hadn't left the editorial on his desk. Either he'd worry, or he'd figure that I'd just given up.

Would he call Gram? Or just back off and give me some space? Why hadn't I left a note for Ringo, telling him where I was meeting Troy?

Because I wanted to surprise him with the scoop, that's why. I wanted to be the big hero, wrapping up the story at the last minute.

Even if Gram and Ringo started to worry, what would they do? Even if they looked for me, they'd never think to search down here.

My stomach grumbled. "Don't start with me," I said to it. I couldn't, wouldn't think about food. I wouldn't think about the fact that tonight was pizza night at my house. I wouldn't think about bubbling cheese. Spicy tomato sauce. Thin, crispy crust.

Okay, Casey. Focus. You've got to get out of here. And if you don't, you're just going to have to sit here all night and build an airtight case against Troy.

Could be a long night. I moved forward cautiously. I had to find something to knock against the door. If the janitor was still around, he could hear me. My hands were tired from pounding already, and they didn't make nearly enough noise. Where was that mop?

Something brushed against my face, and I screamed. I flailed out with my hands, and I hit something. A chain. I pulled.

Dim light from a bare bulb cast a tiny bit of brightness into the gloom. What a relief. Being in total darkness can be a major drag, even for an intrepid girl reporter.

I saw the mop leaning against the wall. I grabbed it and pounded the end of it against the door. *Knock, knock, knock.* I was sure the noise would get swallowed up in that long corridor. Besides, I hadn't seen any sign of the janitor. He was most likely home, eating dinner. Probably pizza. Pizza with bubbling cheese and spicy tomato sauce . . .

I threw the mop against the wall with a clatter. "This is hopeless," I muttered.

Okay. It was up to me to get myself out. But how?

I examined the lock. It was actually a bolt that locked into the upper frame of the door. If I could balance on the sink and stick something in the gap at the top, I might be able to push the bolt down.

An old shovel rested against the wall. The edge was rusted, but it would have to do.

I hoisted myself up on the big utility sink. Balancing on the edge, I tried to work the edge of the shovel into the gap. I gritted my teeth. Metal scraped against metal.

And something moved.

It was starting to give way!

Ka-chung! The bolt slid down suddenly. I teetered on the edge of the sink until . . .

The door flew open and . . .

I flew backwards—right into the sink.

"Ouch!" A painful victory.

Phoebe stood in the doorway. "What are you doing in the sink?"

"Washing up?" I said crankily.

I tried to pull myself up. Phoebe put out a hand. I hesitated, then took it. She helped me out of the sink.

"What are *you* doing here?" I asked, rubbing a sore hipbone.

"I ran into Troy earlier," Phoebe said. "I told him that you were hassling me. And he said he was going to take care of the problem. Meaning you. Something scared me. I mean, the guy is really cold. So I followed him."

"Why didn't you let me out?" I complained.

"Because I lost him back by the pool," Phoebe said. "Do you know how hard it is to track someone through an empty school without them knowing? I had to duck into the gym, and he disappeared. So I checked the storage rooms and the gym lockers. The only reason I came down this hallway was because of the strange noises."

"That was me." I dusted off my jeans. Then I looked up at Phoebe. "What changed your mind?"

"You called it, Casey," Phoebe said softly. "Look, I know I did the wrong thing. But I haven't been able to study at home. Ever since my parents split up . . . well, home has been a disaster area. And I couldn't face messing up in school. And my parents . . ."

She glanced away, not before I saw tears shining in her eyes.

I bit my lip to shut myself up. This was her story, not mine.

"My parents are just . . . When they're not fighting, they're bragging about me. They're sure they've got this perfect daughter. I couldn't let them down. Now they're going to freak when they find out the truth."

"Nobody's perfect," I said. I learned that one the hard way. "I hope your parents will figure that out. And give you some breathing room."

"Yeah," Phoebe said. "I didn't like what I did, Casey. It wasn't me. And letting Megan take the blame . . . I'm ready to turn myself in. And I'm ready to turn in Troy. He knew I was freaked about Lanigan's test. That's why he offered to sell me a copy."

"How did he steal the test?" I asked. "Did he tell you?"

"Are you kidding? He bragged about it," Phoebe said. "He was in the Resource Center when Lanigan printed out the test. He knew it was in his briefcase. Then, in Craft Club, Mr. Lanigan takes off his jacket—"

"—and hangs it in the back closet," I continued.

"Troy stole the keys and opened the case."

"And the Xerox machine is—"

"Right next door," I finished. "Troy had time to copy the test, then return it to the briefcase. Probably while Mr. Lanigan was working on a vase or something."

"It was a cookie jar," Phoebe said. She shot me an admiring look. "You *are* good."

"I'm the best," I said. I just love it when I'm totally right. "So how come Troy left the test in Megan's backpack?"

"I screwed up the first time," Phoebe explained. "When Troy said five minutes before the fourth-period bell, I thought he meant the *start* of fourth period. He meant the bell that ended it. I left my backpack there too early. When I came back, it was empty. I got scared and grabbed it and took off. I thought maybe Troy got caught by a teacher or something."

"So the cubby was still empty when Megan left her pack there," I said, nodding. "So that's why Troy assumed it was yours."

Phoebe nodded. Her tears had dried, but she still looked miserable. I knew what would make her feel better. The *only* thing that would make her feel better. Even though it would make her feel worse at first. That sounds confusing, but sometimes, life just *is*.

I picked up Phoebe's wrist and looked at her watch. "If we hurry, we can catch Ms. Nachman before she leaves. Are you ready to go on record?"

"Well, I have an oboe lesson—" Phoebe started.

I gave her an incredulous glance.

"Just kidding." Phoebe let out a shaky laugh. "I'm ready."

Weasel Boy Sentenced to Math Camp

To: Thebeast
From: Wordpainter
Re: film at 11

Can't talk tonight. I've got a wicked math test tomorrow and got to hit the books. Not to mention write a killer article. Just wanted you to know that Phoebe confessed. Tomorrow, we nab the real bad guy. I'll give you the blow by blow on Sat.

To: Wordpainter
From: Thebeast
Re: update

I had no doubt. You rock. Can't wait for film at 11. In the meantime, remem-

ber this—the plus sign means you ADD the numbers.

To: Thebeast
From: Wordpainter
Re: study advice
Gracias, smart guy.

Early the next morning, I showed up at Troy's locker just as he opened it.

"Guess I must look pretty good for someone who slept in a broom closet," I said.

"Whoa, nothing personal," Troy said. "Just protecting my business."

I nodded. "Then you won't mind if I do some serious sharing with Principal Nachman and the Honor Council, will you?"

Troy looked nervous. "You don't have any proof."

"I have Phoebe," I said. "She decided to do the right thing and confess. Too bad you didn't. Now it's too late."

I reached past him and swung his locker door shut. Principal Nachman stood there, her arms folded.

"Nothing personal," I said. "Just protecting my friend."

◆◆◆

Later that morning I skidded into the newsroom with no time to spare. Everyone was gathered around Dalmatian Station. Toni was clutching photos to her chest, Gary was frowning and Ringo looked up at me, wild-eyed.

"Do you have it?" he asked.

"Just give me two minutes," I said. I sat down at the PC and called up the file.

After Phoebe's confession to Ms. Nachman last night, I had worked on the story at home. Then I brought the disk to school. All I had to do now was add Ms. Nachman's punishment of the culprits. Once Troy was caught red-handed, he'd spilled his guts, hoping to get himself out of more trouble.

Megan was cleared of any wrongdoing. All the kids who bought the test from Troy Chandler would be suspended for a week. Troy would be suspended for two weeks. And everyone involved in the cheating would get an F on the test.

Hopefully, my grade would be a few letters higher. Last night I'd also managed to get in some solid study time, and math was once again starting to click for me.

"Did you reformat page one?" I asked as I sent the article to Ringo's computer.

"I'm trying to," Ringo said. "But Toni won't let me crop her photo—"

"I don't want anybody messing with my work, okay?" Toni said.

"—And Gary thinks his headline should be bigger," Ringo continued. "Except then there's no room for the Simon cartoons. And I really want to run your editorial on page six."

"But there's not enough space, even if you delete Phoebe's article on the debate team," Gary pointed out.

"I've got to get the final layout together in ten minutes if we want to get this puppy to the printer." Ringo dropped his head in his hands. "I can't cope."

"It's simple," Gary said. "If you crop Toni's before-and-after shots, you can make my headline bigger—"

"Crop yourself!" Toni exclaimed. "And let's stick your lame sports story on page four!"

"Quiet!" Ringo cried. "I'm trying to think!"

Suddenly, Megan appeared in the doorway. "Is everything all right?"

"NO!" we all shouted.

"Megan, we need you," Ringo moaned.

"Get your bad self in here, girl," Toni agreed, smiling.

"It's a mess," Gary admitted.

"We just didn't want you to know," I said.

Megan frowned, but I thought she looked a

little pleased. "I thought you were doing fine."

"We tried," Ringo said. "But we can't pull it together without you. What we're trying to say is—"

"Heeeeelllp!" we all shouted.

Megan's frown changed to a dazzling grin. "Okay," she said happily. "Luckily, I'm cleared for action. Let's get started!"

Megan leafed through the articles and photos on the desk, then studied Ringo's layout on the computer. She clicked and moved and resized rapidly. She let Gary's headline go up one point size, and sweet-talked Toni into letting her take just a "smidge" off one photo, pointing out that it actually improved it.

I will only admit this here. Megan O'Connor is one awesome editor-in-chief.

She quickly read through my page-one story, "Cheating Ring at Trumbull Exposed." She looked up at me when she was done.

"Good," she said. "And the way you used examples from another article . . . even a congressman who cheated. What great research! It shows that everyone is tempted. That this isn't just a kid thing or something we'll outgrow. That we have to make decisions about right and wrong every day."

Pride welled up inside me. Okay, Megan was

bubbling over—something that usually annoyed me. But somehow I didn't mind her bubbling over my work. Except . . .

"Megan, uh, about that great research. I didn't have to look far. The author is my grandmother."

"Oh, Casey. But you're the one who saw the connection to what was happening here at Trumbull. Don't run yourself down."

Megan paused and reached for my editorial, called "One Seat Over." I didn't want to admit that I was nervous. But I was.

The cheating ring has been exposed. Students have been punished. End of story?

Wrong. It's just the beginning. When something like this happens, we can get focused on the *who* and the *how* and the *when*. Let's take a minute to consider the *why*.

She could be sitting one seat over. He could have the locker next to yours. And you think, "They don't have problems. They're straight-A, straight-up super-stars. Way popular. Mondo smart."

Think again. They're human. We all are. Everybody is under

pressure. And the easy out is tempting. Between school and parents and friends, the pressure can get pretty intense. What matters is how we act when the choices come down. Sometimes, we make the wrong move. We let people down. We lie, or we cheat. We take the shortcut we know is wrong.

Then what do we do? We blame the pressure. Maybe we blame our parents, or our teachers. We blame everybody but ourselves. But guess what? We made the choice.

And tomorrow, there will be another choice. And the day after that. And after that . . . The decisions we make every day reveal the person we are becoming.

Pressure. Temptation. Easy outs. You deal with it. You try to do the right thing. But you are not alone.

One seat over, somebody else is dealing with it, too.

"What do you think?" I asked Megan, biting my lip.

Megan looked up and beamed at me. "It's just right. It fits in with the pressure angle we have going with Gary's story. The one about that player who's being pushed by his coaches and parents. I say we run it on page two, definitely."

"I'm really glad you're back," I said softly, so that the others couldn't hear.

Megan nodded. She gave me her sentimental we're-sharing-a-moment smile, the one that usually made me either fake a coughing fit, look out the window or insult her. But this time I was so glad that things were right again that I actually smiled back.

She turned back to the computer and began to make the changes. "We'll meet the deadline," Megan promised through gritted teeth.

I should have felt pretty swell about what I'd done. I'd done what I set out to do. I'd scooped my scoop. But somehow, I didn't feel as zippity-do-dah as I thought I would.

I'd turned some kids in. Kids that broke school rules, sure.

I knew that some kids at school would call me a rat. I could take the flak. But I especially hated exposing Phoebe. She was one messed-up kid, but she deserved better parents.

Ringo looked at me. As usual, he was tuned right in to my frequency. "Phoebe?" he asked, and

I nodded. "Look, she did wrong. She deserves to pay."

"I know," I said. "I just feel sorry for her. Once you start asking yourself *why* people do things, everything gets confused."

"Not everything," Megan said. "Phoebe knows she was wrong."

"Maybe this will show her parents how much they were pushing her," Ringo said. "They'll take a chill pill. Let her hang and do pizza instead of oboe and ballet."

"I hope so," I said. "But maybe they'll end up even stricter than before."

Ringo nodded. "Control freaks. I know the type." He gave Gary and me a significant look.

Gary and I exchanged surprised glances.

"Who, us?" I asked, incredulous.

"What are you talking about?" said Gary at the same time.

"Well, duh!" Ringo said. "Talk about pressure. You two have been pushing and pulling at me all week." Ringo hooked a finger into one side of his tie-dyed T-shirt and pulled. "Sports!" He yanked on the other side. "No sports! It was total insanity!"

Gary snorted.

I laughed. "Were we that bad?"

"Who, you guys?" Toni rolled her eyes. "No way."

"I just didn't want you to change, I guess," I said to Ringo. "I like you the way you are. Strange, but true."

"And I thought you just needed a few guy lessons," Gary said.

"Okay, pause for refreshment," Ringo said. "First of all, Casey, people have been trying to change me since Miss Vicki, my kindergarten teacher. Do you think that I'm a piece of Silly Putty or something?"

I grinned. "I guess not."

"And Gary, I've got to bag the balls," Ringo said. "I spaz out when I see a ball. But when it comes to gravity, no problem. I can defy it!"

Gary held up his hands to stop Ringo. "Wait! You're not talking about—"

"I'm trying out this afternoon." Ringo shook out his bandanna and tied it around his long hair. "You are both invited. No hard feelings."

"I'll be there," I said, gritting my teeth. You've got to support your troops, even when they do totally lame things.

"I can *try*," Gary said. Well, it was something. A grudging something.

Ringo turned to Gary. "Besides, cheerleading takes just as much athletic ability as football. Maybe more."

"I have to admit it looks hard," I said. "I saw

it on ESPN. Come on, Gary. Admit it."

Gary groaned. "Why are you torturing me? You might as well tie me to the goal posts and make me watch the marching band rehearse."

Megan spun around in her chair. "Wait a second. I think we're on to something."

Gary looked nervous. "Not the goal posts?"

Toni grinned. "Anybody got rope?"

"Relax, Gary," Megan said cheerfully. "I have an idea for the next issue. Gary can write a column taking the position that cheerleading takes as much athletic ability as football. Then we poll the students to see if they agree."

Toni and I exchanged a smile. We knew having to write that column would drive Gary bonkers.

"I see some great photo ops," Toni said, her eyes sparkling.

"I can do a piece on the origins of cheerleading," I said. I turned to one of the PCs and began to type. "It began as an accessory to a male sport. Today it's a sport in its own right. . . ."

Gary looked anxious. "Megan, don't do this to me."

Megan winked at me. "Gary, it'll be great. Everyone will read your column!"

"That would kick up a real controversy," I said, nudging Toni. "I bet the girls support Gary, and the boys think he's a traitor."

Gary slumped down in his chair until he almost slid under Dalmatian Station. A deep moan emerged. Everyone burst out laughing.

Gary cracked a grin. "Okay," he agreed. "I'll write your *ridiculous story*. As long as Casey agrees to run it on page one."

"A front-page story about sports?" I said, horrified. "Get real."

My Word
by Linda Ellerbee

MY NAME IS LINDA ELLERBEE. I'm a journalist and here's a crucial little piece of my 411: A lot of Casey is based on my life. Or there's a lot of my life based on Casey. You choose.

We're both hard-headed and have big mouths (mostly to cover our shyness). We both see humor in odd places (the world is cracked, have you noticed?). We're both major-league annoying (we would call it assertive). We both want to change the world (who but a dummy does not?). We're both certain we know how (there is no question about this, none at all).

And often we're both wrong.

Okay, so how much of these books are based on my—oh, well, er, um—*life*?

Consider the book you're holding now. The question of what kids will (or *won't*) do to keep from disappointing their parents is an issue in this book and was an issue in my life, but the facts are not the same. Not exactly.

With me it was my mother. I always had my dad's approval. No matter what I did, he thought

I was great, which should have reassured me about me—right?—but no, I merely assumed my father was too blinded by love for me to think sensibly, and so I didn't value his opinion. My mother, on the other hand, was totally hard to please; therefore, I wanted to please her. Regrettably for us both, I seemed seldom able to do so. We were different, she and I, and it would take us years to build bridges across those differences.

Meanwhile, I kept on trying to be more of the girl she wanted, a girl who cared about dolls, dresses, tutus, tea parties and hair curlers—not someone who cared about running with the wind, painting pictures, having adventures, *boys—and* the batting averages of the entire New York Yankees roster. I've nothing against a tutu, mind you; I suffered through ballet classes for years, myself. And I don't really mind dresses (I look totally all right in a pretty dress, even now) or dolls (I will cop to having played with dolls when I was a girl, but at the time I thought I might grow up to become a fashion designer so it was different, okay?). And of course I used hair curlers, we all did. (Tea parties, however, were *so* out of the question.) The thing was, I merely did not wish to be defined *by* these things, or confined *to* them. I was, like all young people, still trying to invent myself. And so we disappointed each other often, my mother and I.

Once, my mother found a poem on my desk in my bedroom. She read it (without asking, naturally), said she *loved* it and told me what a good little writer I was. Rarely had I seen my mother so happy with something I'd done. She assumed the poem, which was about this wonderful, fantastic woman, this perfect *mother*, was about her. *I* had written *this* about *her*? I must be a much better kid than she'd thought.

How could I tell her the poem had been written by a friend of mine, about *her* mother? I'd liked it and asked my friend if I could copy it. I'd actually intended to show the poem to my mother, in hopes she'd see how *I* thought mothers *ought* to behave. But now . . .

Okay, it was a lie not to tell her the poem wasn't about her (and it wasn't my poem, anyway). I knew that. And I knew better. So—did I *ever* tell her the truth? What do *you* think?

Ah, but it's a gray world we live in, isn't it? And just when you begin to think everything is so *simple*, so black and white . . . enter gray.

Take this book, in which there's a great deal of noise surrounding Ringo's decision to try to be a cheerleader. I wanted to tell this story because sometimes the world doesn't seem to make much sense. For instance, have you ever noticed how many of the so-called "rules" about what's considered feminine or masculine are just plain nonsense? When I was a little girl, pink was for girls and blue was for boys and you were never, ever supposed to get the two confused. Then I grew up and the world changed (I like to think I helped). Finally, girl babies could wear pink *or* blue. Finally we had choices. But wait! How many boy babies do you see in pink today? None. So how far *have* we come?

It's not just baby clothes. Today it's fine for girls, big and little, to wear "boy" clothes, such as jeans and T-shirts and sneakers, but how many boys do you see in skirts? And if girls can play with trucks, why aren't more boys playing with dolls? And if girls can go out for the football team, why can't boys be cheerleaders? (I know that in many schools, they are; however, in Casey's school, as you know, there had been only girl cheerleaders, before Ringo.) If girls can do back flips and pyramids and perform other clearly gymnastic maneuvers, why should a boy be thought sissy for wanting to try? Sometimes I feel sorry for boys today. Must be very limiting, all those restrictions.

Do you think it's possible this is what happens when we judge people—boys and girls—by the colors they wear or how they dress or what they play with—or whether they're the right *sex* to be a cheerleader? Don't know about you, but I'm for girls who are soft *and* hard, loud *and* quiet, serious *and* silly—pink *and* blue. And I'm for boys who are the same way. Let's hear it for all the colors!

Oh. One other way Casey and I are alike. We both enjoy a good rant. Thank you for letting me have mine. Now go enjoy one of your own. Get loud. Get passionate. Get real.